Terror On Main Street

Dan J. Pease

Table of Contents

Dedication

Dedicated to Matthew Keatleigh, Rheannon Hanks, Rhiannon Broughton, Hannah Tester, Anna Williams, Olivia Mathewson, Molly Southerland, Harry Munday, Zoe Mangham, Emilia Riley, Katie Pie and Phoenix Blake – the best of best friends. I owe you every success.

Acknowledgements

Dan would like to express his immense gratitude and grateful thanks for everyone who has supported in the production of his second book, in particular, his parents Stephanie and Terry, for their unwavering encouragement, patience and help. Also, his Uncle David for his generous time, energy and artistic stimulation and intellect.

About the Author

Daniel (Dan) J. Pease began writing as a hobby in 2013. Since then, he has written countless stories, fan fiction and ghost/horror novels.

His first published work *'Always Watching'* was published in 2020 and received popular acclaim. It centred around a demonic entity that haunted a young boy called Wesley Devon and those he loved and cared about, revolving around multiple twists and scares.

Dan's other interests are his comedic performances and his passion for acting and performing on stage. He enjoys sci-fi programmes and movies, too.

Dan lives in South Lincolnshire. He attended the local primary and high schools and achieved his BA (Hons) in Drama in 2020.

Chapter 1: The Birth of Fear

Halloween is a scary and frightful time for many across the world. It is a time where children dress up as scary beings: witches, ghosts, ghouls; anything you can think of. We have so many incredible thoughts about Halloween stories.

One of the most prolific places to come alive with dark, scary magic on the night of October 31st is a small village Torquay, and particularly scary is its Main Street.

Many of the most disturbing spooky stories that occur in the chilly area of Devon have spread out to the wider areas of England, rattling even the strongest of bones and making blood run as cold as the water around the North Pole. These stories spread as far as Scotland and Northern Ireland.

Maysville was a reasonable-sized village typically like so many others in England, and Main Street ran the whole length of it. To the passing traffic, it was a postcard-perfect village. At its centre was a square with prominent buildings in each corner. In the centre of the village, it had the customary local shops: a butcher and a bakery passed down through the generations, a quaint antique shop selling vintage items and trinkets to the tourists and a small corner shop selling essentials to everyone.

There was a primary school on one of the square corners, well attended by the children up to the age of eleven. It also had a fierce headmistress who ruled over the school and the children with an iron glove. Attendance was compulsory. No one ever played truant for fear of Mrs. Fletcher's wrath. The children then went to the town of Torquay for their secondary education.

A stone-built church stood at the other corner of the square, which had a generous community parish congregation and a small police station at the opposite end. The police station looked after the community of Maysville and the surrounding villages. It was always manned by a small group of full-time police officials.

On the final corner, opposite the school, was a small public house, which served mostly the village men and passing tourists with beer and traditional ales. The village had a reliable, regular bus route from just outside the station to Torquay and the Devonshire coastline, but most of the villagers had their own transportation. The local garage sold petrol as well as doing small car repairs.

The established houses in the village were mostly from the 1940's and 50's era, but some were much older. The stone-faced buildings had stood the test of time.

The houses all looked alike, apart from a huge mansion house that dominated one end of Main Street. This house now stood empty and was now used as a museum and for some of the local council meetings. The other less noticeable houses just blended into the countryside, their occupants minding their own business. At the same time, the terror stories went on all around them.

Many stories about Maysville consist of the dark, horrific legends that Main Street was built on.

Going as far back as the Middle Ages when 'The Black Death' was coming to an end, there were stories of many infected souls fleeing here from a godless hell, or from the corruption of those in the highest powers, or people abandoned by those they thought were on their side.

It goes without saying that Main Street is one of the most intriguing streets of the British Isles. People have been known to come to take shelter and sanctuary when trying to avoid the dreadful infections of the outside world. But they never had any idea about all the spooky beings that were lurking in the shadows in this village and the supernatural pain they were about to suffer.

Some of the most ancient stories began during the last decade of Roman rule in England. There were many occasions people reported seeing visions of a decapitated Roman army walking down the roads towards a Christian Church, looking to burn it down in the name of their Emperor. Of course, any person who was unfortunate enough to have seen the ghostly army from afar would only have seen the headless soldiers from the waist upwards, given the low hedges and walls lining the straight Roman roads, which were now long gone.

Many people from the outside world heard of this but refused to believe what they were being told. They simply chose to stay away from the deranged area, allowing the haunting madness to spread far and wide until everyone believed the sightings to be as true as solid facts.

The most prolific stories of the haunted Main Street legends extend closer into the Victorian era; an era where Main Street was becoming the heart of torment and a playground for the wealthy. As we've seen, the village of Maysville held a beautiful mansion on the edge of Main Street. A glorious first site for any passing tourist to see when coming to the village. It was certainly a powerful, stately residence, a building so lavish and opulent that not many people received the invitation to step inside the property of such a regal family. A wealthy family owned this mansion, the Lord of the Manor being the richest among them.

He possessed enough money to do whatever he wished, without question or denial. He could influence whomever he wished with his sinister bribes, and he would take no responsibility for the resulting consequences. Anyone would think he was made of money and gold. He was a short, stout man with a receding hairline, thick-set beard, and strange stubby features. He lorded over everything and everyone he owned with relish.

However, his wealth, power, and influence were sadly not to last, and he came to a horrifically putrid end. It showed that even his unscrupulous influence did not offer him protection from chance.

On the night after his thirty-second birthday, on Halloween, after a lavish party where a great deal of wine and food had been consumed, whilst still very drunk, he got up in the middle of the night for a glass of water. He staggered through the great house and was attacked in his own house and murdered by the gloved hands of his poor younger vindictive brother.

It was a gruesome sight for the other family members to wake up to the next morning, seeing the rich grotesque man having had his head cut off with an axe. His headless body was found propped up against the top bannister of the stairs in a massive pool of alcoholic blood. The bearded head of the dead Lord was found at the end of the stairs. His eyes were wide open.

It is said that from that year onwards, every rainy, misty Halloween night when nobody can see for miles, the sound of metal slicing into flesh can be heard around the house grounds. The faded object of a dismembered head can be heard tumbling down the slanting staircase, knocking over the suits of armour like a row of dominoes, the sound becoming inaudible as the head reaches the carpet at the end of the staircase. The villagers liked to share this ghoulish bedtime story with their children as a means to getting them to behave if they had been naughty, telling them the Lord of the Manor would come and get them in the middle of the night if they continued with their bad behaviour. It worked most of the time, even if they never alluded to whether the story was true.

Not much is known about what had happened after the Lord's dead body and the decapitated head were discovered. It is suggested that the rich family had decided to cover up what had happened, writing it off as an accident, not that their accounts were actually believable. Two weeks later, the family left the large house, never to be seen on Main Street and never to be heard from anywhere again.

The glorious house was sold to the highest bidder. It now serves as a museum of classic British history and is often used for council meetings.

But how is all of the ghostly activity possible? Something must have happened on that very horrific night to have caused such a great rush of actions and thoughts by the younger brother. And to have them personified in endless suffering. But what was it? There needs to be so much understood about these graphic stories, assuming that they are true. Many would think they were connected and were forced to occur. Are they right to assume this theory? What would be the price for finding out the secrets of such a horrifically haunted place?

Moving forward towards more modern times, it was now September, in the year 1915. World War I had fully begun across the globe and had made its way to Maysville. This place, near Torquay and across Devon as a whole, played a vital part in The Great War. It served as an important refuge area for those fleeing from enemy planes overhead and protection from being press-ganged into the army against the people's will.

Most of these objectors were rounded up by the end of the year and forced to join the forces, ensuring no escape from the torment of war. It was said that many souls of those fleeing were bound to Main Street, held in agonising torment for all eternity, a true fate worse than death.

It is interesting how many people had lost their lives in the county of Devon, and the various methods of how they succumbed to their shocking fates. The sounds of bullets and explosives poisoned the ears who heard them. When people in Devon spoke their haunting words and gave accounts such as these, many of them seemed to draw recollections of the small fleet of tugboats and naval ships that sank under suspicious circumstances in the harbours and shallows, never to be retrieved from the foul murky depths.

Many theories have surrounded the reasons as to why the ships were sunk on the nights in September. Few people dare to ask, and even fewer can come up with a reasonable answer for why. It was widely suggested, given that these boats were test crafts, that they had fallen apart and were destroyed by the violent weight of the cargo they were carrying. It is not uncommon to suggest that enemy fighters destroyed them; however, the reality remains far more mysterious than this simple suggestion.

A certain clear fact is that many lives were lost on these heavily manned ships. The highest number of deaths in the fleet was said to be 250: Half of those were civilians on the run from conscription and the rest were women and children. Many had families; those families never saw them again, nor did they recover from the loss of those that were cruelly taken from them.

Main Street, Maysville, is a street with many secrets and stories. Especially the gruesome ways people have suffered. But what is it about the street that has caused so much unrest and carnage? The fate of many was never known and often never questioned.

Our real story begins in more recent times. Two decades before the end of the 20th Century: in the early stages of the 1980's to be exact.

It was a haunting freezing night of October 31st when a tragedy struck in the middle of the local church. It concerned the horrifying passing of a well-known young man known as Sean Ethan Michael Diaz. He was a 44-year-old man working for a local barber shop, as a part-time sweeper in the middle of the village, not far from the last place he was seen. He was quite a charming young man with long blonde hair and sparkly brown eyes.

He was walking slowly down a winding path of gravel through a hollow graveyard until he entered the giant church. He threw his cap onto a coat hanger that was beside the door before he approached the altar. This young man, Sean Diaz, died in a most brutal way. He was set alight in the church, burning to death in a fashion that no horror movie would dare display on the screen.

With no one close by to save him from his fiery fate, he burned slowly and painfully on the Holy rug. The scorch marks embedded into it remained visible for several days until it was finally thrown out with the garbage at the end of the week.

Had anyone been watching, there would have been no consolation. It was said that the emergency services arrived subsequently to see what had happened, and they stated that the deathly sights were too horrific to comprehend. Many of them who were there told of how awful it was to see the young man reduced to a pile of singed skin and a burnt cloth of his T-shirt with holes showing straight through. It was such a vivid depiction that people had begun to think the church was cursed, causing many people to lose their faith and walk away in fear for their safety.

The funeral was held in the same church the following day, November 1st; Father Hayden Carrey led the service. He was incredibly saddened by the death of the likeable poor man. Tears trickled down his wrinkly face as he read aloud from the official texts. He blessed those who had come to pay their respects to the fallen boy. There was not a dry eye on the grounds of the church that day.

But the worst of these ghostly situations were about to begin. No one would have any particular clues as to what would happen next, nor could they fathom why he returned to deliver his message. Everything seemed to happen too fast for those intelligent parishioners to understand. But, whatever happened, and whatever was seen on the nights in question, the images certainly left a very vivid and disturbing impressionable picture in the minds of those observing the unwinding future events. And they were likely to cause some horrific putrid nightmares for those who witnessed the events and were touched by them as such. The overflowing of evil was fast approaching Main Street, in the little village of Maysville.

The next day, on November 2nd, the priest arrived at the fateful church to conduct the regular sermon. Father Carrey was incredibly wise for his twenty-six years as a religious figure. He was a tall bearded jolly man in his late forties. Kindness, compassion and genuine care emanated from him, felt by all those that lived in Maysville. He warmly spread his words of advice and care to those in need of it. There were lots of people present to hear his wise words and witness the insane events that followed – events that would destroy their senses of belief and would wreck all ideas for Father Carrey's sense of morality and judgment in this sinister time.

Father Carrey was in the middle of his regular Holy duties, wearing the official gowns and accessories, a mitre covering his receding blonde hair, and reading from his sacred documents when all of a sudden he heard a horrible scream coming from inside his church. Father Carrey looked around the church. His expression reflected angst and worry. He now began to scratch his wrinkly neck. The people in attendance were just as dumbfounded as he was. What was going on? Where was he looking, and what was he looking at?

Then, before the bright blue eyes of Father Carrey, a ghostly figure of a young man appeared to be floating towards the Holy Father. It appeared from nowhere, hovering slowly like a balloon in the wind. It appeared to be real in the flesh, except the humanoid object was translucent, and not flesh at all. The priest wiped his eyes in astonishment, not quite knowing what to say next. He was not sure what he was looking at, even after putting his glasses on.

The figure was standing directly in his line of sight, showing a grotesque face savaged by the flames that had sent him to the grave. The figure gave another impossibly loud scream in the face of the cleric, loud enough to shatter the stained glass in the windows. This scream sent shards of glass onto the ground below the doorway of the church's entrance. The vibrations sent everyone reaching for their ears, clutching them until they turned red, some feeling theirs run with blood at the bellowing sound of the loud scream from the burnt lungs of the spirit.

The priest was startled at what he was looking at, so much so that he grabbed the candlestick and raised it in the sign of a cross before the mysterious apparition with the idea of banishing it. But, alas, this was a futile act. The ghostly human shape remained where it stood. Seeing this supernatural power made Father Carrey drop the candlestick in terror. The ghostly shape moved towards him. All those inside the church could see him too, now.

The charred remains of the young man made him look nearly unrecognisable beyond every human shape. His once golden blonde hair was scorched by the flames that had engulfed him and turned to a miserable grey, granting it a colourless feel. Ash could be seen within the locks of his frazzled yellow hair and burnt bald scalp. Every step that this creature took was a weighted stride against the pure humans inside the church.

His entire skin resembled that seen on a man who's been working down a coal mine for years. His clothes had lost their rich colour during life and were now burnt pieces of rags. The poor man's face had been torn in different directions by the flames that caused his downfall. Several parts of his skeleton were visible, the bones peering through the raggedy clothing, resembling a zombie. The spectre of the torched man was shrouded in a foggy gas, making him as barely recognisable as a scratched and faded videotape.

Seeing the apparition of the burnt man before his eyes had caused the clergyman to collapse in the direction of his audience. He fell into a panicked shock of deranged trauma, leading him to faint, falling forwards onto the new holy rug that had replaced the burnt one removed earlier, the rug where the man had met his gruesome fate. When the cleric had fallen to the ground unconscious, his nose bleeding, the ghost was nowhere to be seen in the church.

Father Carrey was taken away to the hospital to have his wounds assessed and to sort out his mental state. When he eventually woke up in a daze of confusion, he began babbling about what he had seen on the service night. His Churchwarden,

Keith Zorro, tried to reassure his master that he had been in a terrible dream. But there was no way of denying the damage done to his mental health. The story of what the cleric had seen spread like wildfire into the heart of the village until every soul was trembling. The folk of the village were terrified at what they heard. They could not believe something so vile could be true. The story was obscene to unaccustomed ears.

And now it is said, every Halloween night, on the night before (more commonly known as Devil's Night) and over the next two succeeding days and every rainy night when mortal eyes can see nothing within the moist mist, the burnt mangled ghost of Sean Diaz walks again. Like a horrifying warning out in the open. He walks the village slowly and scarily, making a mark, and vanishing into the unknown against a clear black sky with no moon to guide him. He is gone before anyone can conclusively see him, but the villagers feel his presence. It would not be long before he strikes in the most despicable methods possible. When ghosts are undead, suffering is the only thing that fuels their wrath, and all they can do is seek blood in the hope of bringing them closer to peace in heaven.

If people thought Sean Diaz was the only apparition walking along Main Street, they would be proved horribly wrong. Many residents on Main Street could tell you that the village of Maysville was a breeding ground for ghosts. A place where people come to die and be reincarnated into the underworld like Diaz was and many others before him, the Romans and the Lord of the Manor, to name but a few.

Two decades prior to the fiery death of Sean Diaz, another case sprang into existence. The villagers had been happy to write off the past experiences as hysteria, but they would soon be forced to wake up when they realised why they happened. They had no idea that an example had been replicated, and the death of Sean Diaz was the act of revenge against a horrific act that was destined not to go unpunished.

Before Diaz's passing, a murderous criminal killing was committed in cold, calculated blood. A shrewd individual murdered a man known as James 'Jim' Walter Myres after Jim had made the costly mistake of having an affair with the man's sister. That too, on the night she got married to an important rich royal heir of European descent. Word got out about the infidelity, and the brutal murder occurred. The individual had hoped to bury this act of treason so no one would remember.

The killing was carried out when the murderer stabbed Myres in the neck with a serrated cooking knife. Blood sprayed everywhere. With his body still bleeding and his lungs gasping for breath, Jim found himself taken to a nearby river where his vicious killer proceeded to drown him in the dirty waters until the last ounce of life was swiftly taken out of him. He was left to sink to the bottom of his watery and bloodied grave. Stories recounted this dreadful act from that day on, and the villagers called him 'Wet

Jim.'

The man who committed the atrocious act was never caught by the police or charged with the murder. It was thought the murderer had influence and used his rich status to hide his involvement in the dreadful act. The knife used in the execution was never recovered. Jim's body was never found after his death. Many people searched for days and weeks for any evidence of him or his grisly demise. The court's ruling on Jim's disappearance and what had happened was deemed inconclusive, resulting in the investigation becoming cold. There were hardly any words or explanations that people could come up with. So, in time, the death of Jim Myres was labelled as suspicious and extremely inexplicable. Although the events about to unfold are likely to shed a little light, it is unclear whether the resolutions will be clear.

Many observant people around the area of Main Street will most likely give you the warning that whenever the moon is full and purely shinning against the black starry night sky, they have seen the shape of the unfortunate deceased Jim Myres on the prowl. They fleetingly observed him emerging in spectacular and haunting fashion from the river and walking up the bank, the place where he was dragged to his final rest. They have seen a shadow-less figure of a man rise out of the river water. With a knife lodged into his neck, but no blood flowing. This is a time in the world where the dead take their invisible steps into a tormented realm of existence.

Chapter 2: The Nightmare Begins

Haunted by the foundation of despair of the past was the present-day version of the dreaded Main Street in Maysville. Progress paved along with time, keeping up with the technology and architecture of modernity. The new street residents of the street were happy to reside there; happy for it and happy about it. More or less.

Despite the implicit sense of horror about the place, they had been living in peace. They had to pay a great price in order to procure this peace. And like any other generation that made their home on Main Street before them, the present one was soon to be subjected to a torrent of horrors too; nightmares, perils, and terrors to keep them awake at night for all eternity. Like many people that had suffered before in the classic ages, these frightening events would take away everything the modern residents knew. It would wreck their human minds by turning them against each other.

The events of fear began on a misty moonlit night in October. Halloween was a week away. Many youngsters were looking forward to it along with children, eagerly getting outfits ready for trick-or-treating. The village was decorated in the traditional colours of orange and black, ready for the fun to begin.

Everyone was getting ready for the big night, hoping for fun and safety on the popular pagan holiday. They were ready to spook each other out in the hope of creating a buzz, especially with all the sweets involved. There was a young girl working at the local flour factory. Her name was Cameron Sandler. She was a decent and well-meaning girl with short blonde hair, bright green eyes, and long skinny limbs. She had pale skin that was as soft as a sheep's wool. Her family had lived there ever since World War One as part of the war effort. The large flour factory where she worked was on the edge of the village. The factory adjoined the original wooden windmill. Although now no longer used, as the factory had shifted to modern milling over a hundred years ago, the family who owned it had done a fair job at maintaining it. It could be seen for miles in every direction no matter where the village folk stood and made an interesting tourist attraction for those coming to visit the village. The tall sails of the mill had stood proud for many years, but they were not the best of sights given that the wood of the sails was slowly rotting. It made them look visibly gross as in their rotations. Plumes of smoke and flour could now be seen periodically bursting out of the tall, blackened chimney to one side of the main factory building. This smoke would occasionally travel down to the village, engulfing everything it touched with a thin layer of burnt flour and wood remnants.

Cameron had a slim build for a girl who spent her days carrying and decanting large sacks of flour, but she worked hard at her job and was paid well for her efforts, with handsome wages of £50 a day. It was enough to survive on after four days of busy work each week.

On this particular night, Cameron was on a tiring night shift with her colleague, Mr. Michael 'Mike' Kevin Cage. He too was a hard-working individual, significantly older than his younger assistant, with a pleasant personality to be around during the work hours. His light blue overalls always seemed to be covered in the white peppery powder from the flour bags, but he did not care. All that mattered to him was putting in his twelve-hour shift that night, which was required by his employers.

His hairnet and mop cap were seen covering up his bald hair. Anyone would think his hair was blue like his stringy hairnet, covering the large dome. A ginger bristly beard was clearly visible among the khaki colours of the snood covering his neck. His boots were covered in thick powdery flour, making it look as if he had walked through massive piles of snow. It made walking especially uncomfortable.

Both Mike and Cameron had been asked by their boss, Mr. Adam William Fraser, to take a massive truckload of flour to a rival bakery on the other side of the village. It was needed for the large quantities of baking for the holiday food being prepared, as well as for the massive Christmas parties that were being planned and catered for. This included the famed Christmas cakes, buns and loaves of bread that the Main Street shops were world-renowned for. The celebrations were sure to be glorious.

All of a sudden, as the clock struck the hour of 22:00, a large, glorious barn owl hooted loudly in a vine-covered tree close to the windmill. Mike reacted sharply and looked up towards the large bird making the noise. He felt his skin turn cold. His hands began to violently shake as if he was on a zip line. He walked towards a wooden bench and leaned against a brick wall before sitting down on it in the hope of calming himself down.

'What on earth is it?' Cameron enquired. 'You seem rather tense this evening.' Cameron was quite observant. She always took note of people's emotions, and on this day of her nerve-ridden colleague going through tense thoughts. Sensing that it would be time to get going on their important journey, she quickly turned off her mobile telephone and placed it in the pouch of her overalls. She then resumed her attention to the fragile emotions of her work colleague, who was clearly going through some mental turmoil about the movements surrounding them.

'That sound reminds me of something,' Mike gulped, sweating now. 'Whenever that owl hoots like that, there comes a misty fog blowing in around us,' he described vividly. 'Legend tells us that such mist precedes the onset of a ghost that joins it as well. You should take good care on the road ahead tonight, Cam,' Mike warned nervously. He finished his tale with a gulp of fear in his throat.

'Don't be such a stupid wimp, 'Cameron snorted indignantly. 'That's just a pathetic story. It is too early for the Halloween season anyway. Save these for your nephew. He will believe anything you tell him. Remember the time I told him he was adopted?'

'I remember that' her co-worker recalled. 'He was crying for days. You can consider yourself lucky I didn't fire you.' He paused. 'You should not be so flippant, girl. The stories of this village should not be taken as callous jokes. You should respect the village's history, especially stories of 'Wet Jim' and the unexplained deaths of the villagers in years gone by. You never know what could go bump in the night. Especially before Halloween,' warned Mike.

'I can distinctly remember a group of hikers going missing when they visited here last year. The murderer was never found, only a pair of skeletons on the side of the road.' Mike remembered that time vividly, perplexed that the police could find no clues to the mysterious killings. Mike had never described something so clearly in all his life. He held the bottom half of his face in shock at what he had just revealed to the young woman.

Cameron spoke with a sly tone in her voice, 'If you are that freaked out about going out, then maybe you should stay home tonight. '

Mike did not appreciate her flippant attitude towards this sensitive issue but was not tempted to step down. 'Not a hope in hell, young lady, 'he responded. 'I would like to get paid the extra overtime just as much as you. So, we shall both have the privilege of taking this load to the bakery.'

Cameron felt this to be Mike's choice, though a hard bargain. She got into the van along with Mike and they both made their way along the dark country roads. As Cameron looked around the quiet neighbourhood, she heard the same owl hooting in the same tree as before, the same awkward rhythm and sound from its beak. Cameron felt nothing towards the creature. 'Stupid bird, 'she said insultingly.

Moments passed with both of the workers silent on the open road. It was an extremely uncomfortable drive. Mike, who was driving, felt his stomach churning like butter. He tried his best to hold the vehicle still as it bumped around like a ragdoll inside a battered suitcase being carried by a gormless child. Cameron still felt incredulous at what she had been told. 'Hooting owls, foggy mist, spooky ghosts. This village is as insane as the mental asylum at Tattersby Home. The villagers are cowards. I see no mist here. This is all just a cock-and-bull story you would expect to hear at this time of year,' she scoffed.

Mike felt insulted by her dismissiveness. He hated the idea of him having wasted his valuable breath on such an ignorant child. Normally, his powerful, wise voice was well-respected, especially by his managers who always required a good amount of his advice on their projects. However, this was not a normal time at all, given especially the events that were soon about to unfold.

A long boring while later, Cameron would be foolishly proved wrong about her hasty denial in the supernatural.

As the silent shaky drive went on, a thick cloud of misty fog filled the area. It was as cloudy as a bottle of sour milk. Mike found it hard to see around the twisting country lanes. He slowed the van down and cruised gently along the bumpy road, not feeling good inside at all. Cameron squinted her eyes tightly, trying to paint a picture of the road ahead. It looked as if she had gone blind. All of a sudden, they came upon a burning orange light, looking like a fire sprouting from the trees they were approaching. The light was being suspended above the road. Cameron was extremely alarmed at what she was seeing.

'What's that up there?' She cried out. Mike slowed the van down until it came to a complete stop. Mike applied the handbrake and turned off the engine, feeling extremely anxious at what was about to occur. Both people looked closer towards the luminous object.

'It's an amber light,' Mike observed. The light looked like a fire spreading across the branches. 'We had better be cautious around these parts.' He then stuck his head out of the right-hand window. 'WHO'S THERE!?' He called out into the mist. There was no answer. No one replied.

An unsettling silence cloaked the lane. Mike restarted the van and they moved off again. This time, they drove extremely slowly. Almost the speed of a snail. The tension levels were welling up inside the large van. Their heartbeats increased as fast as the bumpiness of the journey.

Half a mile later, more strange objects and images appeared along the narrow road. The van was next made to stop close to a dead oak tree close to the road. It was a dead tree, with branches groaning in the wind. A tall house stood close to it, looking down on them. Cameron looked once more. The tree hadn't grown in years. Its roots had been polluted, rotting it up. She looked closer, she noticed that the tree had a large wooden sign nailed to it. It was written in blood-red ink, saying 'DON'T GO ALONG THE RIVERBANK!' This message was clear cut, displayed in capital letters, and an important warning for those driving on this road, clearly a signal to go no further and turn around. The workers felt it was wisest to comply.

They were both incredibly frightened at what was going on around them. This was the first time they had seen this bizarrely written and irregular sign on the journey through the dark woods.

'FOR CRYING OUT LOUD!' Came a loud outburst from Cameron. Mike jumped at such a loud exclamation from his co-worker. This outburst startled him so much he almost fell out of the vehicle's seat. He considered himself lucky that nothing worse had been uttered by the young girl, for fear of waking up the neighbourhood nearby.

'A little self-control if you please,' Mike exclaimed.

'How strange can this trip get?' Cameron wondered. 'This better not be those stupid schoolboys playing a game! If it is, they'll certainly be facing some angry parents when I tell them.'

'No one has ever warned us concerning the riverbank before.' Mike failed to recall any similar incidents. 'The traffic lights ahead are red. Why would that be? Nothing else is going on now. There is no other traffic coming from the bakery. There's no reason for them to be like that.'

Then it happened. Both of the people gasped at something from across the landscape. An ominous light came on in a nearby house close to the road. Cameron watched in bewilderment as a yellow light moved from one side of the house to the other and up to the next level, to a top window, revealing the thick faded shadow of someone. The human shape moved across the landing of the house before it vanished from view like a lightning strike. The light suddenly faded as if it was fog in spring. The bizarre movements made those inside the van shudder out of control and think unholy ideas at what was going on. For Cameron, there was only one explanation.

'G-G-G-G-Ghosts!' she stuttered in a state of shock and almost fainted. 'You were right, mate. You were right about everything you said. We are in some profoundly serious shit. There is something here. The owl, the mist, everything on this journey. This has to be linked with something. What the hell does it all mean? What do we do now?'

Mike had no idea what this was all about, nor could he comprehend the reality of this situation. He had not thought, in any way, that the story he told had any real foundation. He had noticed, by looking across through the van window, that the sails of the windmill were turning around. They had not done this for a long while. Mike soon knew why.

He cleared his throat, slow enough for him to collect his thoughts. 'I don't know a lot about this, lass. There is something clearly wrong with this place. That bedtime story sounds worse than I imagined. This is enough to make anyone faint from vicious fright: I think it is best that we return to the mill and put everything back. It is way too dark anyway. It's too hard to think.'

'I think you might be right,' Cameron agreed as the light faded away. It was quickly gone and all that was upon the house was cold dark. But this only meant that the haunting figures had only died down. They were sure to make another move.

'We could always deliver this flour in the morning. The manager should not be annoyed if we did it another day. Do you think he'd mind?'

'I'm sure he wouldn't mind a small delay,' Mike agreed. 'He's always struck me as someone with a great deal of patience'. With that in mind, Mike made a U-turn around the creaking lane and drove the heavy sacks of flour back to the mill.

The return journey was taken safely, and the two of them placed the sacks back in a cool area ready for the morning. Both co-workers went home for the rest of the night shaken but none the worse for their fright. They wasted no time in rushing for the safety of their beds in the hope of sleeping off the things they had seen. Getting to sleep was especially difficult given the strange images. They thought about the incidents they had witnessed. What was it?

What was doing these strange things? Why were they occurring, and who wanted them to be seen? Only time would reveal all.

This would mark the first day of the fear and nightmares. The terror had only just begun.

Chapter 3: The Morning Calms

By the following morning, the mist had faded away, and everyone was up and about, working diligently as usual. There came a peaceful day with the boiling sun blazing upon everyone working on Main Street. But, as most people had done regularly, they had reckoned without the mysterious events that had occurred the night before.

Both of the witnesses to the bizarre events, Cameron and Mike, decided to speak with the boss to discuss what they had seen, especially the mysterious warnings that they had encountered on the riverbank and the sightings at the house. It goes without saying that they were seriously disturbed about the last evening's events and had hardly any sleep throughout the night.

Mr. Fraser was an extremely stern but wise man. He had short ginger hair and freckles around his cheeks. He was always impeccably dressed in the latest designer suit, tailored shirt and dark shoes, which had the maximum amount of shine on them. He had a small white cloth in his suit pocket to wipe away the flour dust from his buffed shoes. He did this regularly and with a certain amount of irritation as this occupational hazard spoilt his powerful appearance. He knew everything about everyone who worked for him. And everything that went on around his windmill, the business and the politics of the entire village.

The two workers stood in Mr. Fraser's office. Mike had been in this room many times to assist the boss with his latest project or business deal. The men mutually respected each other for their individual strengths. Mike noted for the first time that Mr. Fraser's office was a large room but sparsely decorated given the man's need for designer status. The room's contents consisted of a large oak desk, strong leather-backed chair and rows of wooden bookshelves filled with files, books, and other paperwork necessary for Mr. Fraser to do his day-to-day business. The two workers stood still in front of Mr. Fraser and recounted the previous night's activities. Mr. Fraser could see Mike was physically shocked by the night's events and although he did not know the girl Cameron as much, he could see she was really frightened. When he had heard the story, he was extremely alarmed to learn of his employee's ordeal.

'You should consider,' he commented, 'how lucky you are. Lucky that you did not go anywhere near that riverbank. You could have found yourself meeting 'Wet Jim.' You have no idea what can happen when he spots fresh blood, especially how insane he has become.'

'I can understand that Mr. Fraser,' Mike nodded in agreement. 'But we have no way of knowing who warned us.'

Their boss was fishing for multiple ideas about these disturbing events. He uttered a strange suggestion, 'Have the pair of you, in any way possible, considered that it might have been an actual someone or something coming from the old house near the tree? Maybe someone who has lived there in the past? Would you not think to ask that person you saw in that house? Did you not think this?'

'We had thought about that idea,' Cameron declared. 'But we cannot be certain. It was night, after all. Do you have any idea who might live in that house?' she asked. 'I didn't think that house had an occupant,' she recalled.

'I think you meant who used to live in that house.' Mr. Fraser moderated his tone and his suggestion in a chilling way. He, as well as anyone else who recognised the importance of the ghostly legends, knew that a house like that had a lot of history in it. Cameron felt very uneasy at what she was being told. 'Now you're going to have to tell us more,' she whispered softly.

Mr. Fraser sat down on the edge of his desk and began to tell a spooky story to his employees.

'We live in a horrific age of ghosts and goblins,' he began studiously. 'People will tell you so many stories. There is a sinister story about a young girl called "Victoria Julia Willis." They call her, "the girl on the stairs," for the reasons I'm going to relate.' Mr. Fraser beckoned the workers who had been standing to sit in the chairs opposite him.

Mike gulped, a severe amount of fear filling his stomach, bringing him even lower than where he was sitting. He felt he had heard this story and that it had tragic consequences for those involved in it. 'Who was this Victoria Julia Willis? What does she have to do with this?' He asked nervously. This was a question he would soon regret asking as his fear began to swell all around his body. He folded his arms and overalls around him nervously as the story was about to be told to him and his colleague. He scratched the stubble around his neck and pricked up his ears in attention.

Mr. Fraser cleared his throat loudly as he resumed the tragic tale of this mysterious house owner. 'Victoria Julia Willis was an important person who lived on Main Street. A councillor with lethal connections with the Supreme Court in London. There was no one she did not know on Main Street, and she seemed to know everything that went on around us. She was known to have a lot of angst with people below her, her tough love always showed it and she always made sure that it worked, regardless of any consequences. If she came towards you and stared at you with her hypnotic green eyes, you knew you had done something to upset her, and there would be extreme hell to pay. And it would be paid through the nose. She once had a head chef sacked for the most appalling service in a restaurant. It was something about an uncooked piece of pork. The outcry was beyond comprehension. I should state though that if she liked you or thought you had some spark or character quality that she would be fiercely protective of you and your family, even if she did not particularly like you.'

'She sounds like a "Female Godfather" if you ask me,' Cameron commented through tense breath. Cameron was not used to powerful people being intimidating towards her, but she was quick to learn how this felt, especially from Mr. Fraser. 'I can't say that I would have wanted to have met her for risk of being sacked like that. But keep going. What is her connection to what we had seen?'

'How did she die?' Mike asked. He was more interested in the back end of the fateful story, rather than who the fearful powerful woman was. 'I assume it was in some unpleasant way. Possibly in that house in the country under bizarre circumstances?'

'You have assumed correctly,' Mr. Fraser confirmed. 'Let me continue.' He straightened himself up as he proceeded with his spine-tingling story. 'It was obvious how Victoria loved to work long hours. I once heard she worked for eighty hours with hardly any breaks. I can remember seeing a large row of coffee cups lined up against a wall. It could have filled ten bin bags. Whether this is a true reflection of her work ethic or not is conjecture, but it sounds right given how extremely tired it had left her after work had finished. One thing is for sure, it clearly contributed to her untimely death.'

'What happened to her?' Cameron asked. She felt as hooked as a fish on the end of a fishing rod.

'It began in the small hours on a Monday. It couldn't have been later than three in the morning,' Mr. Fraser outlined. 'Victoria came home after an extremely late night in the office. As normal, she turned on the light as she walked in the door. She placed her purse under the umbrella stand and took off her shoes. She was fatigued, owing to working late. The light dimmed to a strange shade: A shade that Victoria could tolerate. She made her way to the bottom of the large staircase. Another light was turned on in a separate room, the kitchen. At the same time, the light in the hallway dimmed further until it was almost off completely. The electricity supply is truly dreadful down that neck of the woods. The phone signal was appalling, which was partly why she always worked late in her office. Victoria proceeded up the stairs to the landing.

It was at that point when the tragic accident occurred in her house. A tragic accident that has gone ignored for the longest of times. Many would think she was the victim of a hilarious prank gone wrong, and that she was converted to a ghostly form of existence.

All of a sudden, a third light came on by itself above her head on the landing floor. This light was way too bright for her to handle, blinding her for a fleeting moment that cost her life. She wobbled around the top step, so much that she lost her balance. She then felt the rotten staircase break from underneath her feet, and plunged through the staircase, falling to her death. Her body was found the following afternoon when people had started to wonder if she had disappeared. Her funeral was attended by those she had cared about over the years of her tenure. Her death was shocking to those in this street. I can distinctly remember the tears around her open coffin, dampening the thick velvet suit she wore every day.

It is the ghost of Victoria Julia Willis that floats throughout that house, forever wandering and never getting back to bed. Like she did in life. She now plunges into every darkness of life and shrieks like a lost soul at anyone who wrongs her.'

The work partners were astonished at what had just been said to them by their knowledgeable employer. This was such a harrowing tale for the naked ear to listen to, giving a wilder side to the haunting legends of Main Street. Both Cameron and Mike had no idea what to think. They gave each other perplexed looks and shocked glares, contemplating the horrific way the woman had passed.

It was Mike who finally broke the silence. He took a deep breath and let out a loud cry, 'What the hell is with this place?' He had a lot more control and hardened resolve than his female junior apprentice but was more than prepared to unleash his anger and angst on a subject of great fear in the street. 'Why are we living here?'

'You tell me,' Mr. Fraser demanded seriously. 'Just get back to work. You still have to get that flour delivered. I want it to be taken to the other side of the village by the end of the week. If you do not do it, I will have no alternative but to deduct part of your wages for it.'

The pair of workers walked slovenly away from their powerful employer. All throughout the rest of that workday, the story that they had just learned plagued their minds like a virus in their brains. They thought of how tragically Victoria lost her life. Both of them had no idea that worse was to follow. More ghosts were out there and ready to come out and haunt Main Street into insanity. Considering that the sails on the windmill had now moved in different directions than before, the workers could tell that everything about this was not a sick joke.

Chapter 4: The Next Terror

The workday played out as normal. The workers were still violently shaken up by what had happened the night before.

Now, there was another young lady working with Cameron and Mike. Her name was Taylor Murphy. She was an assistant related to Mr. Fraser, being the daughter of his uncle, so that made her his younger cousin. She was a cheeky young lady of about 34 with beautiful blonde hair and soft, smooth skin. She presented herself as a very firm and confident woman, never shying away from telling jokes and making sarcastic comments.

'You had a weird night, didn't you?' Murphy commented. She was sitting on the wall outside the factory, eating her lunch with Mike. She was eating cheese and watercress sandwiches. He was eating a protein bar and drinking a protein shake out of a flask.

'As if you would believe any of this,' Mike snorted, seething from the stressful conversation taking place. 'There's no evidence of this awkward goings-on. You cannot prove anything has happened to this wreck of a village. People just tell these stupid stories at night and around the campfires on Halloween because they think it is great to make fun of atrocious acts and make them seem as if they were real and actually happened…when of course, they didn't. Where do you think the phrase 'Creepy-Pasta' comes from, sweetness? We all have our own lives outside of our stupid plastic mobile phones and our over-use of television sets. There are more dangerous things than an average episode of EastEnders.

You really need to live a lot more.'

'You've had thoughts and experiences,' Taylor reminded him. 'It was stupid hours at night. You think many strange things then. 'There's a Captain at the police station who seems to have had a few encounters in the past, not that he has spoken much about them.'

Mike had made so many awkward and countless excuses for what had happened to him and his co-worker last night, but there was no point in trying to deny what was going on down that road and what was lurking in the shadows. Just at that very moment, Mr. Fraser approached them at the end of their lunch break with some important instructions relating to the intended delivery last night.

'I have just had an official report come back from up the road at the authorities,' he said. 'Apparently, the riverbank has been checked out by the police. It appears to be in a safe condition, and they have given it the go-ahead for traffic to use it. '

'Are you sure about that?' Mike asked. He felt extremely nervous at this turn of events. He was hoping for a definite closure. If he did not have to go down to the riverbank again, it would be too soon. 'Is there an alternative route we could take?' He asked. Although having lived on Main Street for many years, he already knew the answer to his own question, which was no.

'As sure as this flour makes me sneeze,' came the blunt reply. Mike could not deny the authority behind that logic. 'You and

Cameron should be able to take the load back down that lane tonight if you are early and fast enough. I would like you and Cameron and Taylor to do this for me and get yourself back here before one in the morning. Then you can go home. You can always make up time next week. There'll be enough work for you both.'

This request, or order more likely, made the two worker's blood run cold. 'Mr. Fraser, you cannot be serious.' Mike coughed as if he were having an asthma attack. 'We've told you it isn't safe down there. Do you want us to get hurt? Imagine the lawsuit.'

'That may well be the clear case,' the boss noted, trying to find the narrow-balanced line in this order and the given circumstances. 'But, as a manager who needs that road to be used for our work and my business, and the high payment that this order offers the company, I have no alternative in the matter. I have to take the reporter's word and ask that the delivery goes ahead as it should have done. I am sending both of you out there tonight. I expect you and Cameron and Taylor to be back early in the morning without delay or failure.' He wiped the sweat off his usually calm brow.

'Are you out of your bloody mind?' Taylor blurted out her extreme reaction. 'Do you seriously expect us to go into that haunted territory?'

'If you want to lose a week's worth of wages as well, young lady, you can be suspended for the rest of the week if you want,' Mr. Frazer uttered this in a terrifying tone. He was dead serious about cutting a paycheque, having done it before due to an employee's behaviour during a production line shift last week when he forgot to wear the appropriate safety clothing.

Taylor's tongue fell down to her stomach. 'I didn't think so.' Mr. Fraser growled. 'Join Cameron and Mike after mopping the floors. I expect you to be there too as an observer. If that van returns in any shape other than I see it now, your head will be on the block.'

It was clear that this hysteria was getting to Mr. Fraser, but they all knew he had to make this delivery, or his beloved company would not survive the next few months, and they would all be out of a job permanently. His three employees did not know how much was riding on this delivery.

He walked powerfully away, back to his grand office at the far end of the factory. He had spoken clearly enough to his employees and was not prepared to waste any more breaths on them in pain of replacing them. When he got back into his office, he slowly closed the door making a silent prayer to himself that he had made the right decision with his employee's lives. He reached for his telephone to make a few calls, not really concentrating on them, still troubled by the night's events.

Later the three co-workers sat together. No one said a word about the subject of the ghost's haunting the road for fear of the consequences from the boss and the gathering mass hysteria from those already disturbed. They had had enough bad luck for that day already, never knowing that there was worse to come around the bend at a vicious rate.

Nightfall came. It looked like any other night experienced in the village, all the same, no different. Yet to the three, it felt quite different, hugely different indeed. But it would not be that way for much longer. The hours passed quickly from afternoon to evening until the full moon was beaming down on the people.

The bags that had been loaded on the van the night before remained in place in readiness for their pending delivery. However, there was more this time, and the van was now even heavier. The heavy cloth sacks weighed sixteen kilograms each and seemed impossible to lift, yet somehow the three of them managed. Everyone seemed to be calm as the rest of the night began to play out like a game of poker. All three people felt ready to deliver the load.

All of a sudden, from above them in the night sky, the hooting of an owl in a dead tree was heard. Cameron jumped, almost dropping the water bottle she had been drinking for the last few minutes. Seconds later, there was a loud whoosh coming past, coupled with the roaring of an engine. Only two wheels could be seen and heard, though. Also seen was a man dressed in thick leather and a tinted helmet. He raced past the goods van at a speed that would make Usain Bolt look like a tortoise.

'What in blue blazes hell is that doing out here this late?' Cameron exclaimed, almost losing breath from the quick movements that she had just witnessed. She had almost fainted from the horrific speed of that motorbike. She peered down the road, but by this time, the motorbike was nowhere to be seen. She took a quick deep breath as she took her time when resuming her words. 'Who on earth would be that crazy to ride that two-wheel noise machine at this hour of the night? Doesn't he even actually know where he is?'

Mike sniffed an unimpressed sniff. He was familiar with this type of antics racing around the street. The noise of the vehicle often made him jump when this particular rider was on the road in a violent manner just displayed, especially having been woken by it several times before when he was not working at night. He cleared his throat loudly as he declared the identity of this careless maniac.

'That, I am sorry to say, was Bruce Kenny Stiles. The village bad boy. Or at least he likes to think he is. He rides that loud, ugly thing as if it was his favourite toy. He doesn't care if people are sensitive to noise, like my brother, or if it is when people would normally sleep. Oh no. He will ride that thing until the rubber on his tyres burns and burst into flames. He refills it twice a day as if it was a can of beer. It actually surprises me that he has not been caught for drunk driving yet. Whenever he stops and comes over, I get the reek of something toxic sold at a bar.'

'Yeah, I was just gonna say,' Cameron added. 'At this time at night! Is he high on something?' She was worried at the lengths and measures that could possess someone to race around at that speed. The gas-guzzling noise would be all too familiar on a racetrack somewhere as part of the World Grand Prix. Even with this behaviour, Cameron could tell that Bruce was not professional enough, nor would he be stable enough to take on someone like Valentino Rossi. 'Where on earth must he be roaring to? Is there really anywhere to go to?'

'I think that he is probably trying to get to the nightclubs in the next city before they close.' Mike snorted. 'This is his usual routine most Friday nights. He would hang around there, dance until his legs were like a jellyfish, get as drunk as a dead body and then race down to the local burger joint. He would then repeat the cycle again next week. Surely he must get bored of this. I am fairly sure that I would. I don't know who raised him to be a stupid son of a bitch, but they certainly didn't teach him to behave properly on the roads. Who knows what could happen if he got killed like that?' He trembled as he delivered his last few words, swallowing nervously at the scenario.

Taylor had been watching this whole scene from a distance but had a lot on her mind. She thought it was the most hilarious thing ever. 'Well, would you look at that?' She observed with a sick sense of humour. 'My older co-workers happen to get spooked out by an over-priced toy bike on steroids. Not so tough now, are we?' She giggled like a freaky maniac at the thought of their fears. The pair of workers were not impressed at such arrogant and flippant behaviour from such a young person, who had not been with them the previous night and would clearly have a quite different take on this frightful affair if she had.

'Just shut your mouth now and get in the van, you whiny little dork.' Cameron snapped. She could not think of a better insult, so that was what she left the matter with. Taylor silenced her mouth and got into the van. She felt annoyed whenever she was put in her place. Having been insulted, the young worker was forced to silence her tongue and sit back in line with everyone else. She scratched the back of her soft neck in humiliation. There was sure to be more said to her. Not that she would actually care about what it really meant.

'We are going to do this delivery, get it over and done with like proper workers, and get paid for it handsomely. Then we will get our worn-out ass's home as fast as we can and wait for everything to go back to normal with no questions asked,' Cameron said.

'We will return to our work tomorrow morning, get a handsome paycheque that pays the rent, and pretend that all this freakishness never happened,' Taylor commanded as she started up the vehicle now that everyone was in. 'I'm not scared of anything out there, so don't make this mess harder than it already is. You, yourself, could not freak me out even if you had the guts to go for it. Now stop driving me crazy.'

But Taylor was scared. They were all very, very scared. She could try to hide it all she wanted, but the others already knew it was true.

Shortly afterwards, back on the narrow open road again, it was not too long before the fog returned to the path they were heading down. The van bounced up and down, and from side to side, like peas in a frying pan, as they traversed and approached the same area.

It would not be long before the strange amber light was seen hanging from the very same tree that had been passed the night before.

'OK then,' Mike swallowed hard, the overwhelming amount of fear that was now within his throat. 'Here we go again,' he whispered as he held on to the handle of the door whilst keeping the other hand on the bags of flour and increasing his concentration further. 'Surely there can't be anything else strange happening again,' Mike said to himself as the vehicle kept on going at a steady speed.

The van progressed much further. It rumbled as it moved forwards into the unknown area.

Then, everything seemed to come crashing down in spectacular fashion. Unknown to Mike, as he was at the back of the van, close to the swing doors, a set of traffic lights flashed from green to red, bypassing a normal amber. As before, the sails were turning much faster on this occasion. Taylor had seen these actions unfold in front of her and she had become spooked too. So much so that she threw off her work cap and pressed her pedal down on the accelerator as hard as it would go, hard enough to burn a large hole in the carpet. The very pressure of her heeled foot was felt as the van gathered speed and rocketed down the road at an impossible speed to measure, enough to light up a radar gun.

'Go faster! Go faster!' Taylor screamed loudly at the van's engine. 'There's a ghost around these parts. Let's go! Let's go!' As she screamed these horrific words, the van bumped and jolted around, and the engine roared like a lion at a violent speed.

'Stop! Stop!' Cameron exclaimed. 'What the hell do you think you are doing, you stupid crazy bitch? You are gonna get us killed driving like that!' She protested loudly in the ear of the violently dangerous driver as she sat in the front passenger seat, hands rigidly fixed to the seat frame. She tried to grab the steering wheel as the carnage proceeded around the van. There was no luck in this action as Taylor's hands were gripped to the wheel as tight as a drawstring bag.

Before the young lady could be stopped, the van raced through a crossing, demolishing it into tiny broken shards of wood. From the shadows near the old house, a mysterious figure was watching them race out of control and off to their certain dooms. The van soared around several bends and uneven mounds of tarmac, causing the bags of flour inside the van to bounce all over the place. Mike, from inside the cargo area, was getting knocked from side to side, sending him repeatedly into the bags. Every time he tried to stand up, he was knocked to the floor again. He could feel every bump, bruise, and crash against his sides as he met the walls of the van at every turn. His agony was only eclipsed by the terror mounting in his whole body.

However, there was worse to follow along the haunted stretch. It would have terrible consequences.

Just ahead of the lane, there was a newly fallen tree blocking the road. The tree had been torn down during a recently nasty storm. The head of the oak tree was drenched in the canal. Taylor could see this ahead and slammed on the brakes, but it was too late. The front of the van bashed into the tree. The van turned upside down and toppled down to the canal, half in the water. The engine ceased to run. The silence was deafening.

The three of them were astonished at what had just occurred. Mike emerged from the back in a horrifically dizzy state. He was covered in thick white dust, two of the bags of flour having burst open all over him during the impossible carnage, covering him in the thick white powder that they were supposed to be paid for delivering it days ago. He looked as if he had taken a long cold bath in the stuff. He was not happy about this situation at all and took his anger out on the young lady that had caused the accident, shouting loudly at her.

'Have you lost your mind, you stupid brat?' He scolded. 'Look what you've gone and sent us into! We are trapped in here now. What the hell were you thinking of you idiot?' He had never been so angry in all his life. 'This was a brand-new vehicle rented from a powerful leasing company,' Mike furthered, still in a fit of rage. 'When they find out that it has been written off, we'll be sued for damages.'

'I panicked,' Taylor protested. 'I didn't know what else to do. We're in a hellhole. I am really sorry,' she trembled. Her bravado was completely lost from her. She was feeling incredibly grateful that she and her two co-workers were obviously not too hurt. She gulped as she saw blood running down Mike's face and hairline, but she thought that it did not look too serious. Mike saw her look at his face, and he winced as he touched a small gash on his hairline. 'I'll have a scar to remember tonight's events then,' he said out loud. Cameron appeared to be in one piece, although the silent fury in her eyes was visible for Taylor to see.

'We all get scared out of our minds,' Cameron said calmly. 'You and I are no different.' She faced Mike. 'But this did not have to happen. You should have kept this fear in check and kept us going a little longer until we had reached the destination. But no! You decided that we should rush out of this mess like a herd of elephants in a stampede. And now, look where this has got us— trapped in this stinking watery pool. You have got one hell of a stupid death wish. I will see to it that this damage will be squeezed out of your wages like juice from an orange when the day is out and certainly not ours.'

'Well, that's simply great,' Mike growled. 'Now what the hell are we going to do? This van can't stay in the water for long.'

All of a sudden, there was a cold rush of wind around the three of them. It was sensed through the rustling of leaves in the trees nearby and the shivering of cold skin from those stranded in the body of water. Cameron looked up out of the window. There was a large ominous full moon shining its ghostly white light down from the sky. Cameron knew all too well what this meant, having recognised the signs of the stories.

'Oh God,' she whispered. Everything horrible about the village was about to unfold. 'He's here, 'Wet Jim is here!!!!!'

And, true to her haunting words, the ghostly figure of Wet Jim rose up above the waterline until every last bone of his body could be recognised. He began walking on water towards the submerged van while the three of them sat in a traumatised state. His clothes were ragged and drenched to their once fine stitches. The three of them looked on as the ghostly human pulled a large, serrated knife from out of the side of his neck. Since he had been deceased for many years, no blood flowed from the neck wound as the blade was removed. His broken jaw moved down as he opened his mouth, and it reached as low as the bottom of his neck. He moved his hand to deliver the killing stabs, with his knife firmly gripped in his hand. He towered over the fearful trio, frozen to the spot, unable to move, and held by his ghostly magic. He brought his knife down on each one slowly, making shallow cuts through their delicate skin at first, then thrashing movements up and down. Blood, slow at first, trickled down their bodies, then it began to ooze profusely as the slashing increased in depth and intensity. The blood pooled at their feet, drenching the van floor around them and spreading into the water, turning the dirty water into crimson red. Mike staggered forward, holding his chest, which had been slashed open. He slumped into the water. Then came Cameron, as Wet Jim caught her a savage blow with the knife to the side of her face and head. She fell backwards, clutching her face, blood dripping through her fingers.

Loud screams filled the air until there was nothing. Taylor watched her fellow colleagues drift underneath the waterline, knowing it was her turn next. The dreadful pain emanating from her side and the vicious blow to her head told her she had been his next victim. Then everything turned a dark black cloud of cold unconsciousness.

Chapter 5: Report

Later that same night, many people were still awake along Main Street and in their homes, yet to react to the carnage emerging around the village.

Taylor was the only one out of the trio of workers to have escaped the encounter with the drenched spirit. Not only was she soaked to the bones with the disgusting river water, but she was also traumatised physically, emotionally, and psychologically. She was trying to make sense of what she had seen as she staggered down the riverbank back towards Maysville and into Main Street. It was not too long before her fleeing steps turned into feeble limping amongst the gravel on the road. The purple hoodie she was wearing was soaked with sweat, and her heart was beating like a drum. The blood loss had stemmed to a small trickle, the wound matted to her shirt. Every movement was agony for the poor girl. The gash to her head throbbed, and her vision was becoming blurred.

In the corner of the village, there stood the police station staffed by the most powerful group of police officers that Devon could offer. Men like Nich Love, known for kicking someone's backside for stealing a roll of fruit pastilles from a corner shop. Men like Matt Cruise, known for being both the good and bad cop in the same questioning room. Both men never worked apart from each other and were recognisable for their bristly brown moustaches. And the empowering Police Captain Eddie Maguire who presided over them all with a skillful blend of grit, determination, leadership, and compassion.

It was truly lucky for Taylor that the station was manned twenty-four hours so that she could tell them her story. As the clock struck two that terrible morning, Taylor burst into the reception area, her lungs and legs fit to burst with dread and panic. But, before she could utter a word to the receptionist, she quickly lost her final gasp of breath and collapsed in front of the desk. The receptionist, a tall thin respected woman, gasped at the sight of the poor girl in front of her. She pushed a panic button underneath her desk to alert police staff nearby. Several officers came running to see what had happened; Matt took the soaked girl to a nearby empty cell in the hope consciousness would return life to the girl's body. Nich was assigned to keep watching her and would let them know when she woke up. An ambulance was poised outside to take the girl to the hospital if her condition did not improve.

Half an hour passed at the station; the police team watched over her as if she were one of their own. The girl was breathing normally, and her colour was slowly improving from the ashen grey to a mild blush pink colour. The team decided the ambulance crew was not needed at that time, but they remained on standby just in case she took a turn for the worse. It was not long before the exhausted girl woke up in a dizzy daze. A small, thready pulse could be felt beating on her right wrist as she regained consciousness. She was initially breathing very abnormally, but this had settled and started to return to her normal breath rate and rhythm. Her ears were ringing like a school bell, and her eyes were getting as wide as the banks of the river the van had driven down to the water's edge where the horrific accident had occurred.

Taylor could feel a makeshift dressing on her head and side wound, and she had a fleeting feeling of safety before panic rose in her again. She had the sense of warmth in a dry blanket around her shoulders, but inside she was frozen to the bones, so cold that she felt that she would never be warm again.

'Give her some room, give her some room.' A dark-skinned police Captain forced his way through his associates and took immediate charge of the situation. He handed the girl a glass of ice water as she lifted herself forward. His name was Edward 'Eddie' Maguire. He had a bearded face with short deep brown hair, a gold stud earring in his right ear. He had strong arms and large hands, which had clearly seen many years of service. He was wearing a light blue shirt with a grey tie, with a plastic nametag attached to his top right pocket. He pushed through his fellow troops to inspect the traumatised witness.

'It's OK,' he said calmly, looking directly at Taylor. 'You are safe now, surrounded by kind people. Tell us everything slowly and calmly, take your time, and take the water to steady you. Take it from the top.'

'I-I-It was down by the river,' Taylor stammered, trying to choose the best words to describe the actions. 'I saw this guy come out of the water. I watched him brutally stab two brilliant flour factory workers that I was worked with and had started to care about. There was blood all over the waterline, on him, Mike, and Cameron, who he had just attacked.' Taylor thought to herself for the first time that she did not know their surnames or very much about them at all, but she remembered that Mr. Fraser would know all the necessary information. Taylor then continued relating her story. 'The guy then dragged them both down under the water. They all vanished from the view. With no other options, I just scrambled to the riverbank and pulled myself out. I only just got out in time. With nothing else to do, I ran and never looked back. It all seems a blur.'

She began to think of a familiar story. 'I think it may have been Wet Jim in that river,' she could not believe she was saying that.

Captain Maguire's aghast face said everything. It said it all. He removed his glasses in horror as he wiped off the sweat beginning to build on his large forehead. Every other member in the station was feeling the same as they backed away in terror. He felt extremely nervous about the situation and the ideas racing through his head. It was a very sinister thing for everyone to sleep on. The frightened girl then collapsed back into Maguire's strong arms, the tears uncontrollably falling onto his blue shirt. Taylor cowering into his arm, finally absorbed the reality of what she had just witnessed, realising she would never be the same again.

Within the next couple of days, the story spread across the village, with all the residents of Maysville and particularly Main Street becoming aware of what happened; the disappearance and presumed deaths of the poor people involved.

The police, under Maguire's direct supervision, had conducted a vast search of the area, though no signs of any dead bodies were found. The news was incredulous and spread infectiously along the street. The wise Police Captain thought that the road along the riverbank should be closed off in order to prevent any further loss of life. To any average authority, this would seem like a normal response to tragic events. But, of course, Maysville was not a normal place for normal thoughts to originate. As no one would listen to the Captain, he shunned his ideas about the ghosts in public and continued to advise the use of the perilous road.

The riverbank road, therefore, remained functional as if the pair of tragic workers had not met their fates in the first place. However, taking advantage of the ignorance of the street, Maguire took a short trip down to the river. He pulled up a couple of yards away from it before disembarking down the wide rickety lane. He gazed out to the body of water. He looked down the lane with narrowed eyes. His silhouette was highlighted by the moonlight. The water then began to ripple, although nothing had been thrown in it. Maguire saw the ghost of Jim Myres rise from the water. It was covered in old bloodstains, fresh from the attack it had committed. Maguire waded his way into the water and stood face-to-face, directly in front of the phantom. He bravely stood his ground. The water was freezing, numbing every part of his body. The bottom of the river was strangely firm, as if he were standing on concrete. He was surprised how much this interested him, given what was standing opposite him and the story the terrified girl had recounted to him days earlier.

'We didn't want anything like this to happen,' the Captain spoke in a low controlled voice. 'We've been hurt just as much as you have. No one wanted for you to be tormented in this watery pool. There is no shame in lashing out against your traps and evils, but that does not require death at the same time. What happened here was just a plain ridiculous accident that should never have happened. Don't make this any worse than it already is. You could walk away from this place. No one would have to know or get hurt anymore. Surely you can find some peace.'

'That is not possible for a being like me anymore,' the ghost spoke in an Irish growling tone. It staggered towards the brave Captain with a twisted glare in his eyes. 'I have been abandoned in the afterlife just as much as I was when I was a normal man walking around in normal humanity. Resting in peace has not been allowed for me. Life for you mortals has already become worse. The terror on Main Street has only just begun. I will come for everyone who has denounced me as part of the race of the undead. The people of Maysville and Main Street's ignorance will be their downfall. The fear they exhibit will be delicious to eat. I take immense pleasure in knowing that this world will be a new breeding ground for a war of all against all. First, you will take leave of your senses, and then, once you have torn each other apart, my race will take you down in anguish.'

'Race?' Maguire asked in confusion. 'You call yourselves a race? As in a species. You cannot be serious.'

The Captain stepped out of the knee-high water and knelt down gently onto the oily grass. He put on a set of steel glasses around his eyes and took out a notepad and pencil from his top pocket. He wrote down several notes, taking a written description of the phantom standing in front of him using a thick pencil. He gave his long neck a scratch with the end of the pencil when he paused from writing.

'Indeed so,' Wet Jim confirmed slyly. 'I am as serious as the souls of those I claimed last night. You should know very well that there are more apparitions like myself. I will gather them all together. We will rise as powers like the world has never seen. We will take over this puny neighbourhood. It will be infected with our hauntings and fearfulness and all the possible sufferings ever designed. The contagion will spread far across the world that chooses to ignore us, enough to destroy the mentalities of the ignorant. There are so many haunting brothers and sisters ready to be united.'

Maguire could not deny what had just been said by the ghost. He was clear in his mind that this was a serious threat from the undead phantom. But even he knew he could never fall for such fearsome threats from this shadow-less foe. He opened his pocket to pull out a tiny green sweet. He placed it into his mouth and sucked on the juices in it in the hope of calming himself down. He then swallowed the confectionary item down into his throat and gulped it down with a large number of uneasy feelings. He then decided to speak again.

'I'm not scared of you, Jim.' He uttered calmly. 'I'm not afraid of this. I can fight against things like this.'

Wet Jim was enraged by what he heard. He made vicious growls at the policeman but knew that he could pose no threats in his ghostly transparent form, especially with the lost ability to touch someone. However, he knew that this man's time to suffer would come around. And so, before he faded away against the moonlight as if he were the invisible man, he hissed these words to leave a resounding impression. A sentence that made the blood run cold of the most hardened cop that was standing in his eye-line.

'You will be fearful. You will be more scared than you can possibly imagine.'

Maguire swallowed a small amount of fear along with another sweet that he had placed in his mouth. This time a purple one, blackcurrant in flavour. Getting up, he turned on his large, heeled boots and walked away back to the police car on the banks. He lumbered into his car and drove away from the river, taking a final glimpse in his interior mirror to see Wet Jim slowly descend into his watery grave. He placed his foot flat to the floor, and his car tyres screeched with pain. Dust and debris flew into the air as he left without uttering another word. There were very tense feelings around the street everyone lived with, feelings concerning what the street's future could be.

Chapter 6: The Decisions We Make

Soon, many people were asking about what Taylor and Maguire had come across and what had happened to the young workers on the dangerous night. The terror and haunting ideas had truly gripped the whole community and had sent it into an unmeasurable turmoil. Many people were planning on moving out of the street to more distant, safer locations.

One such family had moved up to Somerset. Many others had decided to reach further across the UK, to as far as London and Birmingham, moving in with family and friends, anything to get away from the dreadful village. They would be safe for a brief time. There was no feasible way anyone would take their chances at staying put. In many cases, it could be forever. Who could tell how long this carnage would last?

Captain Maguire had no alternative at this point. He had given the final order that the riverbank road should be closed down immediately. He had advised that the bizarre objects found on the road leading up to it be seized and taken away as evidence. That way, he hoped no one else could come into contact with Wet Jim, or any other ghosts outside of the street, and meet a fate worse than death.

Of course, if you had been paying attention to this story, you will know that Captain Maguire has reckoned without Sean Diaz's ghost that inhabits the church where he was burned to death and would soon regret not taking note. Maguire had been digging for cases across the village and from its history. He had learned about the headless Lord and the boats that were sunk during the war. He hoped that they would provide some foundation for an explanation and help him resolve this and restore some order back to this quiet spot in Devon, but he wasn't confident.

Captain Maguire found that he had the backing of the village senior standing Councilor, Kirsten Farrell. She, like everyone else, believed in Jim's murder. She had heard of the stories; Sean's fiery demise and everything else that everyone was talking about, beyond the shunning of stupid rumours and dreams. She had seen the families devastation of those killed on the riverbank and was sickened to her stomach but was uncertain if there was a true link with the historic ghostly tales and their deaths. To her, it seemed incredible that this could be happening again and now.

Many people believed that this was a very desperate time for the village, going as far to suggest that it was cursed. There was extraordinarily little that people could do to quench their fears of confronting the paranormal.

It was early one morning. Late Autumn was just settling in with the display of multiple leaf colours pouring in all over the trees. Councilor Farrell had met with the police Captain within the village's local public house located at the other end of the village. She entered the establishment to see the Captain sitting in a large booth in the corner of the pub. He had ordered half a larger, granted that he was not officially on duty that day. Farrell ordered herself a glass of Pepsi Max, given her hatred of alcohol, and sat down on the barstool facing the Captain. She opened the top of her blue shirt to cool herself down.

'You don't really think Taylor was telling the truth about what happened on that night, do you?' She asked. 'She could have just been another drunk on her way back from the pub, and only required a night in the cells to sober up.' Farrell felt very sceptical about what had been seen, especially the sinister rumours being spread across the street by the village's people. She was starting to think that this was all turning out to be a stupid joke, a waste of time she could not afford right now.

'Do you think there is any validity in this? 'Is this some kind of joke, a prank gone wrong and the two met their deaths in some other manner?' she asked, dreading and desperate for the response at the same time.

'I think so,' Maguire agreed. 'She's seen something important connected to the hauntings of this village.'

The Captain made his point of view noticeably clear through the serious glares in the features of his face, considering the events of his own spooky encounter with the very same spirit days earlier. 'I have seen my fair share of crazy moments throughout my life. London was such an insane place to work in with all the dangerous criminal activities, hence why I left for the countryside. There was one instance where I almost got killed in a knife fight with a sadistic serial killer. He almost slashed me up. It was only by the grace of the Lord I escaped in one piece.'

'Is that so?' Kirsten looked interested. 'I guess the torments have followed you back'

'Yes, Ma'am,' Maguire agreed. 'London was where I started out as a policeman. It's where I graduated from the police academy. There was so much carnage going on around the city. Drugs, poisoning and murders, almost 70 in one week alone. My Chief had me removed and transferred down here to Devon for my own safety. But it seems to me that hell is breaking loose once again. Now I am paying the price.'

Kirsten decided to flip the subject. 'Captain, I cannot seem to find any concrete answers from anyone in this village. All I hear are stories,' she declared. 'If this carries on, the wider world will think we have all gone insane. What do you think we should do, Maguire?'

The Captain felt very uncertain as he replied. 'Jim did say that there was more on the way, did he not?' He recalled bluntly. 'It is clear we should get ready for when they come for us.'

'Give me a break, Captain,' Kirsten snorted out in disbelief. To her, this idea of an undead invasion sounded like the stupidest thing ever. 'What on earth do you think they can do to us? They are ghosts, for crying out loud. If they touch you, they will go right through you. The same if you touch them. What do you have to be afraid of? What kind of harm can they do? It's simple physics and clearly common knowledge for those who want to dabble in the dark arts of contacting apparitions.' Kirsten felt convinced by what she was saying.

'They're more powerful than you think, Councilor,' Maguire declared. 'You cannot possibly imagine what these things are capable of. I can only dread what they will do to us in the near future.' He flexed his broad chest as he breathed. 'It has only just begun.'

Kirsten sniffed loudly with a worried expression on her face. She knew better than to make remarks like these, especially as she was in over her head like everyone else in the village. She gulped as she decided to show a lot more respect from then on, given how the conversation was likely to proceed. However, this respect would soon be wasted on the ideas that would be formed.

'Did you reach out to the relatives of the victims?' She asked. 'How did they take the news of what happened that night? Not well, I would assume.'

'Yeah, that's one of my responsibilities. I met the families and told them the news,' Maguire confirmed with a sad expression on his face. 'Cage's and Sandler's families were horrified when they heard the news about their death's in the river. Heartbroken and destroyed when I told the news of their demise and how that came to be. I could barely stay in their house's when they all started crying. It is just as well that I did not mention any thoughts on them being taken by ghosts. It is bad enough to lose family at a time but even worse like this.

'Farrell, I have a kid sister called Julie. Seven years younger, to be exact. We grew up together in London and moved across the country together. She is everything to me. She is the best thing to have ever happened to me.' He coughed loudly before proceeding to ask an important question. 'Do you think that you could grant me your word on something?' He was asking her to keep a firm promise.

'What would that be?' Kirsten enquired. She leaned in further with intense listening. Her blonde hair glistening by the window's light, her bright blue eyes open wide, giving him her full attention. She was immaculately dressed from head to toe and clearly took a great deal of time and pride in her appearance. Maguire quickly thought to himself, she was a uniquely beautiful woman, before sharply refocusing his mind on the subject in hand. She gathered that this would be part of an important instruction about to be given to her by the police officer. She was quite good at listening to the authorities. She scratched her smooth neck as she waited anxiously at what was going to be entrusted to her knowledge.

'If anything happens to me, you must not tell her about it. Whatever happens to me in this escapade must be kept a secret.' He made his controversial deal clear. He could remember vividly what happened whenever his sister was told horrific news; her grief and sadness could be overwhelming and lead her to extremely morbid thoughts. He was desperately concerned that his own horrific fate could lead up to hers too. He did not rate his chances of escaping this terror on Main Street, especially with how shaken he was ever since the girl burst into the police house.

Kirsten nodded her head in great acceptance at the policeman's request. 'As you wish, Captain.' She agreed to honour this demand from the officer to not pass on any tragic details to his sister. She had met her before when Maguire first came to the village, and she was quite a pleasant person to get along with. His sister was quite a small young lady. Her smile was strong and sincere, visible against the freckles on her cheeks. Anyone would think it was superglued to her face from the day she was born. Kirsten snapped back from her memories. She felt that she needed more things to be done concerning the pending disastrous issue. 'What else do you think we need to carry out?'

Eddie then made a very thoughtful face as he wiped the sweat from his forehead using his clean white handkerchief. There was an interesting idea that had swarmed into his large mind. With no concern, he voiced it. 'It would appear,' he theorised in his mind, 'that the safest method to controlling these spirits and protecting ourselves would be to close the church as well as the river.'

The Councilor was shocked at such a controversial suggestion from the officer. She pushed her glass away in intrigue. She felt that there was to be more of this demand, and the reason behind it. Maguire continued his theory further.

'I would suggest this course of action, regardless of how controversial it is, because I do not want to run the deadly risk of any other people meeting with Sean Diaz and succumbing to horribly fates. He had heard the stories of the sighting of Diaz and felt the church was his focal point. It is the same as Wet Jim down by the river. From what I can gather, these ghosts are horrifically volatile and prepared to kill anyone who dares to cross their paths. That is not a risk that we can afford to take with the people of this village. Public protection will always be the most important part of combatting these foes.'

Kirsten felt incredibly nervous at what was being suggested to her and the whole direction of this conversation. She felt that this was indeed a controversial statement to make and agree to despite her tremendous power, authority, and influence. She knew very well that not everyone would agree to this sudden change.

'I do not reckon that Father Carrey will take very kindly to hearing something like that,' she warned. 'He'll think it's all just a massive ploy against the moral rights of the church. You know what he is like on accounts of superstitions and myths in this village.'

'You think the village's morality hasn't been damaged enough?' The Captain questioned. 'How many more people do you or they want to suffer mentally and physically because of some invisible/visible apparition. How many more souls would you think Father Carrey wants to lose to these unwavering ghostly beings? Where do you find the balance? Try answering that one, Ma'am.'

You would not probably think it to look at and to listen to. Still, Captain Maguire actually appeared to be the most switched-on individual out of the pair of people sitting in the corner booth of that Devon public house, especially in such a strange situation concerning spooky ghosts and the drastic measures they had to take. It was keenly noted, obvious indeed for those patrons who were close to the bar, that the careless neglect of those less versed in ghosts, led people to their doom, ultimately losing lives to the fearsome apparitions and bringing ruin wherever they haunted.

Seeing this as inevitable, Captain Maguire got up from his seat and walked away from the pub in silent thought.

Chapter 7: The Church

The moonless night spread invisible shadows across the streets, buildings, and the cars left on the Main Street. A biting freezing wind hung in the air, chilling everyone to the bone. Soon, the ghost of Sean Diaz would be awoken once again. The night was soon to be spoiled with the blood of his victims. The week had been horrible. There was every possibility life was going to get worse before it got better.

Captain Maguire was taking his scheduled ride across the village. His lights on the front of his police car were the only way he could see ahead. He was riding shotgun, and carrying one on his lap, with an associate driving next to him. Her name was Katherine 'Kath' Scott.

Kath was a junior member of the village police force. She had only just started to get used to driving the unmarked police car around the village, as well as the other duty vehicles they. She was a petite woman with shoulder-length straight black hair, which made her contrasting pale face and bright brown eyes stand out even more against the night's mist. She pulled up in a safe place as Maguire swallowed fear down his throat. He removed his seatbelt and got out of the car. He breathed with a cold sigh of dread as he looked towards his young ward.

'Wait here,' he whispered. 'Sean and I are going to have a little chat about the events that have been going on in the last few days. There's a great deal of things that I have to say about what has been going on.' He gulped once again. He craned his head up towards the towering church building. It was like looking at the house of a giant. He could barely make out the top of the haunted church tower among the cold dark clouds. It was hidden within the misty clouds in the heavens above them, a mist that was swallowing the Main Street as if it were a sinkhole in the ground.

'You would be a lot better off talking to yourself.' Came Kath's poor attempt of humour at the situation. She gave a creepy snigger at what she had just blurted out, thinking that it was such a hilarious joke. Kath thought she was a funny person, thinking that she had the right to jibe. This was not everyone's opinion though, and her timing could have been better, yet she did not think about it.

'That isn't funny.' Maguire frowned. 'You will never progress anywhere with comments like that.'

The Captain turned on the heels of his thick black boots and walked up the gravel path of the church. The chilly wind was whistling around his ears, and he rebuked himself for forgetting to bring his winter gloves and scarf. Everywhere he looked, there were headstones all around. He felt they made the scene feel a lot spookier than the atmosphere the ghosts had caused.

He reached out a broad hand towards the door handle. He twisted it and pushed his way into the church. He only had the last dying hours of the evening before the church was to be closed down. He entered the church with more fear in his stomach than his dinner and his throat went tight with the increasing anxiety he felt.

Inside the church it was incredibly cold, even colder than outside, Maguire thought. The only light in the vast place was coming from the altar – a mere candlelight burning on its last ounce of wick. The Captain removed his cap and placed it on a hat stand above the door as a mark of respect for both the Lord and the phantom it held. He walked along the new holy carpet towards the burning light. He tried to make out the outline of a human shape against the altar. The solitary human was draped in clothing torn by the flames of hell and hissing like a possessed snake. Maguire kept advancing until he could make out the ghostly shell of a body, at which point he came face-to-face with the horrific spirit. He gazed at the being as if he were looking at the Grim Reaper in the eye, seeing the death in him.

'Diaz, can you hear me?' The Captain fought back his dread as he tried to communicate.

'I hear you, and I can understand your human voice.' The phantom responded in a deep, whispering tone. He sounded like he had a cold and was coughing through every other sentence. It twitched its head as if it were cracking its long bony neck. It spoke some more to the policeman.

'You cannot deny our existence forever, officer. There is no fooling who we are and what we can do. We are as real as you humans. It may be even true to say that we are more human than your pathetic flesh and blood. We will take this planet by force by any means necessary. You will be our eternal servant for us by the end of our campaign.'

'That may be the case, Sean. But you forget who is alive in the room,' Maguire declared. The Captain liked to think that he was being smart in some way through the use of his cheeky remark. It would not do him any favours. Maguire was soon about to have a costly realisation that his ridiculous jibe would have the most horrendous consequences whilst he was there. 'Can we not talk like civilised beings?'

The subject quickly morphed into a different matter entirely. 'Are you part of that clan of infidels that would wish for us to be condemned to the fires of hell? And be forgotten by a wasteful society?' Sean asked suspiciously. 'They have been part of our existence for many generations. Being dishonest about the ghosts that haunt this small village, brushing us off as frauds. They waste their time trying to deny the facts that are obviously true.' He had now turned one hundred and eighty degrees, now facing away from the policeman. He did not wish to look at the mortal man, to avoid undivided eye contact for as long as possible, not wishing to be disgusted. He paused for a reply to his accusing question to the Captain.

Maguire knew he had to be honest with the apparition. 'It would be pointless for me to deny your existence. I am not as blind as everyone else. I have not been here in this place as long as everyone else. All that I can promise is that I don't mean you any harm at all, Diaz. You were a rising person in the village with so much potential. You deserved better. Everyone deserves better, no matter what they look like.'

'That is hardly true. For you, for me and for everyone,' Sean retorted. 'You are a fool to think I can believe everyone in this society is good and pure. We both know that that statement is a falsehood. You are a simple policeman who would happily sit by and allow the living to make fun of me, deny the existence of the undead and fill the world with evil. You would allow me to play tricks on those brainless sheep, like that idiot Bruce I picked on in the supermarket. This corrupt place will pay for what it has done to me.'

'No one wants to die like you did Sean,' Maguire pleaded. 'Please turn around so I may see your face. I feel silly looking at the back of your neck.'

Sean recognised this request from the policeman as a serious command. He rightfully obeyed it and turned to his right so that he was standing parallel to the man in the middle of the altar. Maguire was moved by the ragged and mangled appearance, the burnt clothes and the burns and tears all over his translucent skin. There was hot red fire in his eyes. The very fires of hatred and evil. The same type of fire that cauterised the boy all those years ago.

The Captain started breathing strangely. He had never seen anything this repulsive since his days in London. He gulped loudly once again. This image would be imprinted in his memory forever.

'This is what I was reduced to,' Sean described. 'No one believed Father Carrey when he told his story about me. He called me 'The Unholy Ghost' at my funeral, describing the method of my passing. Yet you decide to believe I am real. It makes me wonder why.'

Just then, there came an uninvited guest. Maguire's associate, Kath, had been creeping up from behind him whilst this was going on. She had been just behind the half-opened door, listening and taking down every word that was spoken. With no regard for her or anyone else's safety, she kicked the church door fully open and burst through into the centre of the room. Captain Maguire turned to see her rush in like a bull in a china shop.

'GET OUT OF HERE!' He yelled across the church floor. 'GET OUT! GET OUT NOW!' He screamed.

But the fateful action had already occurred, and the warning had been given too late. 'You dare disturb my audience, wretched unbelieving child!' Sean Diaz's spirit raged furiously as his supernatural state began to build up inside the church. 'Your intrusion will be your downfall, girl, as you taste the fury of my powers and become an example to those who cross my threshold where they do not belong.'

Kath took one look at the ghostly spirit, and she screamed, joining his to create a noise loud enough to make the stained-glass windows shatter. Shards of the window rained down on top of her and the Captain, both people being cut by the fallen debris. Kath began to shake violently. She felt her body fall apart and turn to ash and smoke, as if she had been dowsed in a flammable liquid. Her last breath frazzled as it left her mouth. Captain Maguire was aghast at this ability and rushed over to her remains. There was nothing but dried-up scraps of bones crushed into dust.

The whole execution of her death made the Captain incredibly angry. Angrier than he had ever been in London. He turned back towards the murderous spectral villain. He made a murderous glare of his own, as if he were about to punch the creature to death. Of course, this would have been a pointless act to think of, let alone try. But the Captain definitely knew this ghost had crossed an unforgiveable line.

'I hope you're proud of yourself, Sean,' he said as he began to berate the ghost. 'That was an uncalled-for attack. She was only a young girl.' Maguire had only known the fallen officer for as little as a few short weeks. Training her may have been a persistent bore, but she meant well, and was capable at her job and had had a lot of potential in the police force. Now that potential future was nothing but a pile of dust on the stone floor.

'She deserved that. She deserved to die,' Diaz growled furiously. 'Everyone in Mayville and here on Main Street deserves to die for their sins that go unpunished by you useless mortals. The way I was destroyed and left to be forgotten by such a society. Even worse if necessary.'

Maguire breathed deeply. He made a lethal promise. 'Alright, this is your very last chance. Leave this world of the living whilst you are still free to do so. No one will ever try to deny your existence anymore or try to take you down and disturb you like this. You have my word, and it is as solid as ice. If you do not, there will be no choice but to destroy you and send you back to hell where you belong. If you want us to suffer, you do so at your own costly suffering as well.' This threat was declared with the utmost sincerity and determination by the brave officer.

Sean glared as his ghostly figure began to fade. 'So be it. Until the next time.' With that, he faded against the altar, leaving the shaking distraught Captain alone, devastated at what he had just witnessed.

Chapter 8: Carrying On

The rest of that night felt just as horrifying to Maguire as the way Main Street did in the daytime. The crime scene team had taken what seemed to Maguire an age to collect samples, take photographs, and take his statement. After finally completing his own report and all the endless paperwork, he visited Kath's devastated family. This was his least favourite part of the role, but he knew it had to be done. The girl's mother fell backwards into the chair as he recounted the story of her death to them. The look of sadness on their faces would remain a memory he would be unable to shake for an exceptionally long time. He finally went back to his house at the edge of the village, where he made himself a sandwich, but nausea rose in his throat, and he was unable to stomach even a small bite. Once in bed, Maguire found himself waking up every hour with nightmares and horrifying visions of what he had been forced to experience in the church that night.

By the time dawn was breaking, he was a mess. When he eventually got up after the screeching alarm clock had sounded so many, many times, he staggered his way into the police station. When he entered the office, he informed the Councillor and Taylor what had happened the night before. Both women were sick to their stomachs, just as much as he was, as were the family of his young charge, he recalled, who was flooded with brittle unquenching tears.

Maguire walked around the street. He made notes on his reflections and what he felt about the place. These notifications can be found in the torn, weathered fragments of an old diary that Maguire kept under his bed. These were the thoughts he put to paper:

'This is a place of brutal conflict with itself. This village has been doomed to hauntings since it was first created. People are losing their minds over what has been declared. It is almost like the people in the village and in Main Street itself are at war with themselves and each other. This village will fall apart even before Diaz returns. Yes, he could have his war. But it is doubtful if he would ever win. It is not like we would ever have a chance ourselves. We are in the middle of nowhere at the bottom of the country.

If only we knew what we were up against. We should have been far more educated about these ghosts. There has been a fair share of hardships in the past centuries. Maybe this destruction of Main Street is how it all ends. Even in fires of hell. Rejoice the powers.

After this vital time to himself with his diary and upsetting time to mourn over the loss of his colleague, Captain Maguire and Taylor made their way to the head office in the Main Street police station. In it sat the unflinching Police Commissioner Brendan Thorpe. He was a large man with fierce flexed muscles. He ruled the police department with an iron-clad fist, covered in tightly thick gloves. Maguire nervously knocked on the door, and they were allowed to enter the office of the leading police officer. They were invited to sit down by the superior officer, doing so whilst keeping an eye on the official. Maguire informed the Commissioner of the events encountered over the last few days.

'It is my official police demand that the vile church is to be pulled down to its bare bones and foundations,' the Commissioner responded. 'This may be a cruel idea for the right to worship, but I feel this is the only way to prevent that manic spirit harming another living soul. We have lost great members of our community in the riverbank and the church. I feel that destroying the church will be the first step towards the contagion of this force.'

'Are you serious?' Taylor exclaimed in stunned amazement. She had been invited by Maguire to the meeting to share her story of the night on the riverbank. 'That church is a valuable place of worship. It has been a symbol of Maysville's history since it was erected in the Middle Ages. It ought to be left as it is. As a pillar of our community. As strength against everything that troubles this fair village. As a reminder that there is always hope behind all of this torment of hauntings. Surely you want that for the safety of this community.'

'Not if you want another person to be burnt to death by that horrific ghost,' the Commissioner declared fiercely.

'And let's not forget that the church is a place of worship,' Maguire said in defiance. 'Father Carrey will strongly forbid it.' Although Captain Maguire knew that this ghost had caused havoc in that temple of worship, he still felt it had a right to stand tall.

'Said the guy who had this same suggestion a little while ago.' Commissioner Thorpe retorted gruffly. 'A police officer who does not obey his own word is not one to be trusted in our community. You, of all officials, should know that. Since you cannot make up your mind clearly about the church, I have decided to take over from you and make up your mind for you. My decision to destroy the church is final. This is my final word. I have spoken!'

Maguire knew that whenever this phrase was spoken by the fearsome Commissioner, his orders were a fixed, blunt and intractable law.

He rose from his desk and walked powerfully away from this bizarre debate with the officer and witness, making the floor shake with his tense authority. He reached for his telephone and made the call both individuals were dreading. When he had hung up the phone back on its holder, he revealed that a selected task force had been assembled in less time than it takes to boil an egg. He would join this team. All three of them headed for the church.

It was time for dangerous action to be undertaken. Both of the individuals were angered. They ran after the empowered Police Commissioner. They had a nervous feeling that things were about to turn extremely ugly for this high-standing officer.

Taylor was immediately proved correct, especially with the large angry mob gathered around the police at the church. The priest was standing above everyone as he would do in a prayer session. It was clear to everyone in his presence that he was not prepared to comply with the Commissioner's demands. The Commissioner advanced forward with hazard tape. The clergyman barred his way. 'Get away from my church!' He barked with anger at the Commissioner.

'You have no authority over the law, clergyman.' Commissioner Thorpe hissed like a snake at the religious figure. When he stood against the Father, he towered over him like a tree over a mere human being, his arms as thick as the very branches. The Commissioner made the point thoroughly clear, and if Maguire knew anything about him, he knew that there was no changing his direction once he had made his mind up.

'The law is the law and must be executed as such,' the Commissioner said. 'This has to be done in order to save this village from being overrun by ghostly undead.

'Now, if you know what is good for you, you will get out of my way or feel a different type of chain around your wrists and a huge fine that even your holy Lord will not bail you out for. Obstructing our work is a criminal offence, and you will suffer for it.'

'You have no right to do this.' Captain Maguire came forward so that he was between his boss and the religious man. He held his hands toward both people in the way of preventing them from tussling in the eyes of the public. 'CAPTAIN, GET BACK!' Taylor warned as she joined him. She held onto his arm but was shoved away by the officer. 'Stay back, Taylor!' He warned. 'This is not going to go well.'

'It is out of the question and an unprovoked assault on the house of God,' Father Carrey judged. 'God created this house to be a place of rest. It should be allowed to stand where it is, and you will have no powers to take it to the ground.' To prove the vivid point, he walked back quickly to rip the key out of the door lock. To everyone's shocking repulsion, he gave a clicking sound within his teeth to summon a nearby dog that was close to a tree. He shoved the key into the dog's mouth.

'Try and get inside now,' he scoffed. 'Can you go and force the undead away now? I see it as impossible, and these police efforts are a waste of time.'

'How can that be the case if the dead won't go to sleep?' Maguire asked. 'You answer me that. And another thing, you just broke another law by making the dog devour that key. It is called destroying evidence. At least try and make yourself protectable.'

Father Carrey was having none of this debate. He was not interested in being told what to do by the police officers.

'The matter is closed; the police are not coming anywhere near my church with their destructive materials. If they want God's house to be pulled to the ground, I suggest you come to the altar and take it up with him. I can strongly predict that you will have a field day with the Lord as the press is due too. And the Lord will come out on top,' he predicted as he began to stride away, feeling noticeably confident with his defiance.

Thorpe was growling furiously. As the churchman turned around to go back to the church to conduct his services, the Commissioner ripped Maguire's gun from his holster and raised it to the Father's head. He cocked it and presented it above his ear. He held his nerve as tightly as a weight in a bodybuilder's large hands. The cleric felt the pressure of the gun. He knew that the trouble of this situation had multiplied tenfold.

'Why don't I send you to go and have a word with the Lord in person, Father?' He threatened dangerously. He held the pistol as tight as a wrapped parcel.

'You wouldn't dare,' Taylor gasped. There was no denying that he was deadly serious that he would pull the trigger on the weapon.

The Father turned around to face the Commissioner again. The gun was now pointed towards his left eye. Maguire was aghast at what was going on. This was the worst display of police brutality he had ever witnessed. He demanded to be heard by those ready to take each other to the grave. This was not the function of a policeman when it came to the phrase 'to protect and serve.' How did threatening death uphold the law?

'This is wrong, even for you, Commissioner. I could testify and have you fired quicker than you can pull that trigger,' he warned.

'I wouldn't think so, Maguire,' the Commissioner sneered aggressively. 'You are in no position to make demands to your superior officer. I could send you to meet your maker as well if you want. Anyone would think this trouble was made up by you. Ending you right here and now would end this stupid insanity. I'm surprised you are still here when you couldn't handle the carnage in a major city.'

Maguire turned towards the Councillor who had just joined the dreadful scene. 'Kirsten, where is your voice in this?' He asked. 'Surely you can do something to quash these actions. Tell the Commissioner that he is being unreasonable to these parties concerned. Tell him to back down and come to his senses.'

'They've all got important points of order,' the Councillor recognised. 'Given the authority of the police, I'm afraid I have no choice. I am sorry about this, Father Carrey, but I am afraid Commissioner Thorpe has the right and the upper hand in this debate. Therefore, the church will have to come down. I have no alternative; the people of this village are the main priority in this matter.'

'I'd rather see you all in hell!' Father Carrey roared furiously. He was having none of this outrageous conversation which he felt was just a waste of his time.

Before anyone could stop him, from out of nowhere, and without a second thought, Father Carrey's Churchwarden, Keith Zorro raced forward to protect the Father. Zorro had been the Churchwarden for thirteen years. He had a pivotal role in the church, leading the pray meetings, Sunday schools as well as his church care-taking duties. Zorro was a small man, with brown hair and a handle-bar moustache. He also had a gold tooth which glittered in the sunlight. His family had originated from Cuba, and they had lived in the village since they had moved to the UK in 1962 when Keith was born. He had been watching the whole thing from the sidelines. He kicked Brendan in the chest, making him fall to his knees. He grabbed the gun as it fell from his gloved grasp. He fired the weapon twice at rapid speed, once at the Commissioner's backbone, paralysing him. The second bullet struck the Councillor in the left cheek and the side of her face. The officials were left writhing on the floor in agony and in a massive pool of red blood.

The gathered crowd was enraged and aghast. They had never seen such a vile display of violence and bloodshed, especially from a man of peace and God. The respect for the devout Churchwarden had evaporated in seconds as the Commissioner shook in pain and screamed in horrific agony. The flour factory boss, Fraser, came forward from the edge. He landed a massive punch on the Churchwarden's jaw, sending the Churchwarden flying and more blood gushing from his mouth.

'Are you out of your mind?' He bellowed. 'Is that what you want to teach our children?' He landed several other fierce punches on the Churchwarden before he himself was dragged away and swiftly calmed down by the rest of the police trying to keep the peace.

'Get hold of him!' Bruce called from the back. 'He's just as bad as the crazed policeman.' With this, and ignoring the taunts of the overseeing crowd, two officers Nich Love and Matt Cruise, arrested the Churchwarden, placed tight handcuffs on his wrists and forced him into a police car. These footmen to the Commissioner snarled at the man they had detained. They clambered into the car in the front seats after they had lifted their fallen boss onto a hospital stretcher.

'You're gonna burn for this,' Nich stated. 'The Lord's not going to provide an alibi for this mess.'

'You'd better pray for one of his famous miracles,' Matt added. 'You are going to need one to get away from this life sentence.'

These taunting words rested on the ears of the Churchwarden as he slowly hung his head away from the flashing cameras. The police car was driven away at maximum speed before anyone else could add their own opinion on this matter. Taylor and Eddie disappeared into the crowd as well so as not to be tied up with the massive brawl any further than they already were. There was so much happening at once in the neighbourhood, caused by the hauntings of the village. There was far worse to follow for those who were in the presence of this violence.

Chapter 9: Further Discussions

As usual, with these kinds of horrifying stories, there is always bound to be consequences and travesties for those trying to find a better ground in tense situations.

The events of the past few weeks had shocked the village-like electricity through a plug. Everyone was shattered at the very thought of one of the village's most prominent religious figures having been arrested for the shooting offences he had carried out, even in defense of his employer. Keith found himself to be viciously questioned by several police members over his actions whilst he was awaiting his trial.

It was not too long before he was brought before a packed courtroom. The council chambers had been converted for the trial. An authoritative jury of peers ready to decide his fate, and in front of the presiding Judge, Tobey Justice. The public gallery gave him the most disgusted looks of anger and disbelief. His mentor, Father Carrey, looked at him with the most horrified glares, close to tears in his old eyes as everyone was called to 'all rise,' as Judge Justice appeared in the courtroom and sat above everyone else. His court official called out the case number as everyone was called to order.

Keith felt extremely frightened at being prosecuted for the actions he had committed, especially as a man of God and a high-ranking member of the community. His act of violence certainly went against every moral thing he had watched the Father preach on Sundays, and now he was paying the price for it in the cold, unforgiving hearing. He was lucky that a sympathetic attorney known as Irene Wilson was willing to represent him. Although, she did not feel confident about the events of the court case and the potential verdict.

The testimonies of those who had been the witness and Commissioner Thorpe were serious and valid for the jury to register.

Fortunately, it was both the chilling accounts of Taylor and Captain Maguire who gave substantial evidence for the defense of the Churchwarden. They cited the facts that Maysville and the Main Street had been plagued by ghostly actions since the birth of the village and that the acts of the Churchwarden were self-defense against injustice. With this historical background and a plea of self-defense in mind and diminished responsibility, the jury had no choice but to declare him not guilty.

Many people who witnessed the case were incredibly surprised and relieved that their Churchwarden had been acquitted for such horrific actions towards the police and those in higher powers. The Churchwarden was led out of the courtroom by those who had defended him and instantly sent on his way back to his religious duties. He left with a smile on his face, confident in the knowledge of what had been said to defend him, heading back to the church and the clergyman that he had and always would proudly defend with his last faithful breath.

However, it was not all going to be good news for everyone

around the street, especially those in power.

Commissioner Thorpe was livid at the idea that an attempted murderer had escaped justice. Especially the fact that one of his own had the audacity to defend him in full view of a superior. When Thorpe had returned from the hospital, bound in an electric wheelchair, he wasted no time in reprimanding and firing Eddie for what he had done. He decreed that Maguire be stripped of his badge and police status. He was subsequently kicked out of the police station by Nich Love, straight onto a cruel, unforgiving pavement as a warning to others.

The Councillor also acted with the wrath still in her head. After she had had a significant amount of facial reconstruction surgery and had returned to work, Kirsten had both Taylor and Maguire barred from the council, revoking any further contributions that they might have had in any decisions in village affairs, and ordered that they be shunned in public by all other citizens.

Father Carrey was extremely lucky that his Churchwarden had not been given a lengthy prison sentence for his actions. Judge Justice was glad the law had been administered in this particular way. However, there was an enormous amount of fear of the backlash that was bound to follow.

There was a great level of hope lost among the masses over the last week. Now, with the destruction of morality, all bets were permanently off.

Knowing what could happen, the Judge decided to take a long

break from the law and take a long-overdue rest from his judicial role. One evening, he was in the public house where Maguire and the Councillor had discussed and shared information on the ghosts. He was drinking his usual cranberry juice. The weather outside was extremely cold, a temperature that would have frozen the blood of any man ill-dressed for the season. The terror on Main Street was well and truly known.

It was not too long before the disgraced, former police Captain entered the public house in his rags and tatters. He looked awful as he staggered into the bar. His former uniform shirt had been slashed to ribbons by order of Commissioner Thorpe as a mark of humiliation for speaking out and was now stained with watermarks and blood. There were several tears, burns, and loose ribbons all over his shirt and trousers. He limped slowly over to the Judge and sat opposite him. He had asked for a pint of lager. He stared at the old man across the small table.

Maguire had decided to discuss further theories and ideas of how to deal with these haunting spirits.

'So, where do we go from here?' Judge Justice asked the damaged man. Like everyone in the street, he was insistent on getting answers as to how the terror was to be handled. 'A shit storm has been built up around this village thanks to the last few weeks.

'Distrust for everyone is vast and powerful. The ghosts of the fallen still continue to thrive around us all; please tell me you know what you are doing.'

Maguire knew this to be true on account of the week from hell that he had suffered, eventually leading to the loss of his employment. 'I guess we will have to wait around and say a prayer of hope,' Maguire sniffed. 'Hope that we can deal with these horrific spirits and earn our peace the hard way. There's something else in the distance.' He put the rim of the glass to his lips and downed the amber fluid into his mouth quicker than he could swallow it. He put down the glass as he finished the swig, giving a quiet belch under his alcoholic breath and saying, 'Excuse me,' as he relaxed. He swiftly wiped away the froth from his chin using his dirty hand as he returned to focus on the case. It was time for the story to develop with more deadly secrets. Normally he would have been more prepared for the following information, given it was easy to learn about the decapitated rich man and the previous encounters. Now, this was no longer the case. If the price of interference could not be paid by ignorance, it would therefore have to be paid through the use of knowledge in order to vanquish the undead hordes of pure evil.

'Do you know what is happening?' Maguire asked. 'Do you know what they are planning?'

The Judge cleared his throat. 'There was a horrific death of a lady that was known as Jennifer Diaz. Her demise was truly tragic and dire.' He noticed the eyes of Maguire twitch in recollection. 'Does something there cause a concern?'

The former Captain nodded coldly. 'The surname Diaz. I have heard it too often recently around this village.' He then proceeded to scratch his head with great thought processing. He seemed to recognise that spoken name from somewhere but was not entirely sure about the origin.

Of course, all of us in witness to this tale know it is already the surname of the man in the church. Yet who else does it belong to?

'I can understand that,' the Judge considered. 'Jennifer was the twin sister of the ill-fated Sean Diaz. I knew him all too well. I met him several times when he owned part of the area. I'm not kidding, curiosity got the better of me, and it wasn't pretty.'

Maguire could feel the plot in this mystery thicken like a large wall made of bricks from a builder's site as he inched closer to the informant. He sensed a salty verbal resolution coming a mile away, knowing the extent of who was involved with this appalling case of lies and deceit. 'What does this sister have to do with this case?' He asked. He elaborated this statement with two more questions.

'How come no one has mentioned her before? What on earth happened to this woman?' He asked.

The Judge coughed loudly as he began to relate a further story to the former policeman sitting with him. He beckoned the disgraced officer forward, pointing to his right ear in addition to hear the putrid tale about to be told to the former cop. He placed a bottle of water in front of the disgraced police officer just in case he needed it to calm himself down at the hearing of the divulged information. He could sense that what he was about to say was going to force a vast amount of fear to swell up inside the once confident policeman.

'Of course, it was the bastard Sean. He killed her. He murdered her in the most destructive way he could come up with,' the Judge began.

'He lured the girl down to a lonely part of the country lane, only to ram into her with his car. It was something big and lethal. Possibly a jeep wrangler. The time of death was registered to be at twelve in the morning. I suppose that grants a new meaning to the well-known phrase 'things that go bump in the night.' Maybe you have heard that phrase before. After what I am unfolding here, you will probably not believe anything you hear again.'

Maguire gave an unsatisfied smirk. He knew that sounded corny, but it was not worth revealing or reacting to.

'You can make that awkward face all you want, Maguire. It would not make a difference in any way. The girl is dead. The body was horrifically mangled by the weight of the crash, and she died on impact. Her chest was cracked open and torn apart. Her internal organs were crushed inside her body, like garbage inside a removal lorry. It is natural, yet unnatural at the same time, for being rammed against a signpost at such a massive speed. Her body was crushed to pieces. Her bones were shattered with no signs of life remaining. I almost think there was nothing left that resembled a body.'

Maguire raised his bushy eyebrows at such a thought. He could picture the accident as it was described. It sounded horrific.

'If you think the horror ended there for Jennifer in just being hit and mangled by a car, you would be wrong.' The Judge declared. He cracked his knuckles underneath the desk. 'It was only just beginning for her mangled remains. It may answer the question as to why, when you go to the local cemetery, why you will not find her name printed onto a headstone, especially when you find out what he did with the corpse.'

Maguire raised his eyebrow once again. 'Do you think you could answer some things first?' He asked quizzically, rubbing his hands together to quell as much of his nerves as he could never mind that they were as shredded as dismembered paper.

'What happened to her?' And then he added, 'Who was it that killed her?' He was secretly hoping he could arrest the person involved if, of course, they were still alive in any viable way, in the hope of getting back whatever honour there was left to salvage from his disgraced name. Sadly, now he knew that, even if he put things right in Maysville, he would still be a figure of persistent ridicule.

Before the Judge could respond, he asked, 'What would provoke them to commit this kind of atrocity?' He had to know everything about this case, even when it came down to the basic motive so that all the evidence gained was air-tight, tighter than the largest drums to be played inside an operatic theatre.

The Judge registered what he had been asked. 'I can answer those questions in that very order most definitely,' he declared. 'Pay close attention. Jennifer was going to expose her twin brother for his crimes against her lover: Jim Myres, a name that will be familiar to you.' Justice declared. 'Unfortunately, her nosiness cost her very life in the most brutal way imaginable, and it was taken away by her own brother in a murder made to look like an accident. Everything was planned to the last moment, and it went unnoticed.' He reached into the pockets of his large coat and pulled out shreds and sheets of paper containing documented evidence of this impossible case.

'What more can you tell me of her brother?' Maguire asked. He coughed loudly into his hands as he sat up straight.

Judge Justice described him. 'He was a ruthless character, Sean Diaz. He was so horribly opinionated that would often result in him being shunned in public. He cared about no one in his life except for his own financial gain.

'In his twisted mind, the only real person he felt meant anything to him was himself. He needed to silence his twin sister before she could tell anyone about his despicable crimes that would most definitely send him to prison for life. He didn't care for consequences and took the matter into his own hands and performed the ultimate execution to remove the horrific evidence and prevent his downfall.'

'How did she know it was him?' Maguire asked. He felt something had been leaked for her to uncover the truth of this crime.

'Apparently, she had seen the whole thing through a crack in a wooden door. She was discovered spying on him from afar, and she ran for her life. The brother knew she had to be stopped and silenced. If she told anyone, his life and liberty would have been in ruins, disintegrating his ultimate corrupt power. And so, he killed her in the way I described. By "planning" the car accident,' the Judge declared. 'But there was more to that act of destruction.' He gargled his throat in a loud strange manner. Maguire could see down inside his mouth, which made him feel quite nauseated.

Maguire's eyes widened at this revelation. But the Judge was far from finished with his intriguing story. 'Suffice to say, the killer was believed to have done some seriously disgusting stuff with her dead body that no horror movie would show it.' He pulled out another documented piece of paper showing a copy of a crumpled diary entry, writing in a runny fountain pen. It described the methods used to kill the woman.

Maguire was beginning to feel extremely nervous at what was being detailed. He felt his body shudder in the cold biting wind.

'Would you care to find out what he did to that of his own flesh and blood?' The Judge asked with a breaking voice. He raised his arm and snapped his fingers, demanding immediate attention from those around him. The barman hastily responded to this authoritative gesture and proceeded to pour them more drinks to quench their thirst. He was then forced to go away at the second snap of his thin spindly fingers.

The former police captain wanted to deny him the pleasure of the rest of this story, but he knew that the answers to his questions needed to be heard. So, against his better moral and mental judgement, he nodded slowly before weakly opening his mouth to say 'Y…Y…Yes.'

The Judge put on a pair of his glasses and began a horrifying description of what happened to the body.

'Very well, son. The brother dragged the girl's dead body into a large vat containing a thick corrosive nitric acid. When he placed her lifeless body inside the tub, it began to boil and burn up like the sun on a hot summer's day. Her flesh was simply melted away. The flesh was peeling away like the outer layers of the very planet we sit on, only a lot slower. It crackled like the wood on a living room fire.

Very soon, Jennifer's murdered body no longer resembled a human being, nothing more than a shop mannequin that had not been dressed in a month.

After the body was stripped of its flesh, he quickly fished it out of the corrosive tank using a metallic hook and dried it with the best type of agent he could find. After the remains were clean and dry, he chopped the bones into small pieces, limb by limb, every piece of gunge and residue, and everything else that could be used to uncover who the girl was, even after the acid bath was washed away. That way, there would be no use of DNA tracking.

'What happened to the bones was bound to get even worse. The killer then weighed the chopped bones down with enough weights to be found in a gym. He then placed the bones and internal organs in black bin liners and dropped them into the river that Wet Jim makes his residence.'

'Had he finished with her then?' Maguire gulped. The descriptions of the body's disposal were getting too much to cope with.

'No,' the Judge denied. 'As far as he was concerned, he had only just begun with the destruction of the evidence. Clearly not shying away from breaking every law in the book. He went back to the river and pulled the remains up to the surface and took out the organs. Only the mangled bones were left, and he subsequently took these back to his mansion and burnt them all in the grand fireplace of the large, impressive dining room that I referred to a moment ago. The classic way of disposing of evidence, and no one would ask any questions.'

Maguire was now incredibly disturbed by this latest information. He had seen some abysmal atrocities in his police career, from emaciated drug users to the tortures of the innocent, especially with his time in London many years ago. But what he had learned, and was about to learn, had reached a new level of repulsiveness. He was quite surprised how he had not vomited at what he had heard already.

'W…W…What happened to the rest of her organs?' He stuttered, trying not to choke on his own words.

'The organs were disposed of in two hideous simple ways by two different things: a dog and himself. The organs became his dinner for that night's dirty dealings, making him now a cannibal as well as a murderer,' said the Judge.

'The dog ate the remainder for his disgusting meal.'

Maguire shuddered at what had just been said to him. He looked as if he was going to faint on the bar's couch and vomit on the floor at the same time. He tried taking a few long breaths in and out in order to relax his mind. This did not help so much. He had no idea what was lurking in the dark of Maysville and Main Street. With everything terrible about this spooky story making his emotions bubble up to the top of his windpipe, he could not control what was to come out of his mouth. He took a gigantic breath of angered air and blurted out his disgust in the most verbal outburst he had ever managed to build up inside his mind and inner organs.

'What a dirty bastard!' He almost shrieked. 'A lot of this must explain how this guy never got caught.'

'Oh, there's so much more to this than you can possibly think, my dear boy,' the Judge stated. 'Yes, he was never caught. But that was mainly due to the fact that he had died less than a week before he could be detained. In an act of revenge.'

'Yes, well, I think that I have heard enough,' Maguire snapped in defiance. 'I'm out of here now.' And with this, he made a massive leap up from his seat and ran his way towards the door. He raced as fast as his legs could carry him out of the public house. His drink was now spilt on the carpet. The glass was now lying on its side under the table, the half-full liquid inside now staining the pub floor. It was quite a dramatic reaction coming from such a figure who had held a position in authority.

The Judge sat there as if nothing had happened. He smirked as he downed the last drop of his drink. He watched the former Captain leave in shock. 'Oh, get ready, sonny. There's a bigger twist in this tale on the table that you just leapt away from,' he said to himself in reaction to the bizarre actions of the escapee. 'Who knows, you might actually prove useful for something once in your life.'

The Judge then went back to drinking his drink, only to feel a serrated knife being stabbed into his neck. He choked on the oozing blood that had started to trickle around the inner wall of his throat. It then gushed into his mouth and poured out like a waterfall. He breathed his last breath as his body fell on his side on the sofa he was sitting on, dead in cold-blooded murder.

The knife used to kill him was drawn from his punctured neck by Commissioner Thorpe's henchmen, Nich Love and looking on was Matt Cruise. He wiped the fresh blood off the blade with a napkin soaked in a nearby bucket of water. He then handed it, by the hilt, to the Commissioner, who looked rather satisfied with the action just committed. Thorpe was now sitting in a wheelchair after the horrific events played out at the church. The man smirked as he placed the knife away from the newly murdered victim and tucked it away from view in an inside pocket.

'Thank you, Nicholas,' Brendan said. 'That's one loose end we can tie up. Now for that trouble-making ex-cop.'

'He's told him about the story,' Love commented. 'He'll blurt out everything about how this place was built. All the power and connections with the rich and the government. Our very existence will be crushed if he spills the beans. He'll ruin everything.'

'Certainly,' Thorpe sniffed. 'Well, you had better go catch him then. He's a fast man. If he spills it, all the power that we have built up in this village will crumble like a cake. The Lord of the Manor's foundations would be for nothing. All our arduous work and connections will be broken. You'd better catch him before he tries anything stupid.' With these orders, the troops went out of the bar and ran after the former cop. The Commissioner wheeled after them, biding his time.

A sinister plot was brewing in the world of Main Street. The forces of evil were on the move. The treacherous Commissioner and his two henchmen paid for their drinks at the bar and made their way out of the pub after their former colleague.

Meanwhile, Maguire had run as fast as he could. He was still physically shocked at what had happened in the last few moments.

'This is some scary shit,' he said to himself. 'I need help with putting an end to this nightmare. I have known this from the whole time these ghosts have been here. It is clear that I cannot handle this mess on my own. I need to put together a team.'

With this in mind, Maguire set himself to run around the village in the hope of putting distance behind his attackers and gaining members of the public to join in a team to fight against the struggle that had plagued them and ignited the terror on Main Street.

Chapter 10: The Fight With The Undead

Maguire was certainly not the type of person to give up quickly despite the torrent of bad luck he had suffered over the last few days. As he had expected, he could see the sails on the windmill turning once again. He had not run far when he reached several people standing around a burning garbage bin. They were Taylor Murphy, the motorcycle rider, Bruce Stiles and the flour mill boss, Adam Fraser. The trio was alarmed as the disgraced policeman coming forward to plead with them for their help that they fell rapidly silent.

'Guys, listen please,' Maguire pleaded. 'This terror on Main Street is driving people insane. The spirits are going to take this place down. And us with it.'

'Why should we believe you?' Bruce asked. 'You got your boss crippled by your stupid interference. Anyone would think that you have gone as mad as these ghosts around this Main Street. Who's to say that you would not turn on us as well and feed us to this undead army?'

'It sounds weird, but you have to believe me, Bruce,' Maguire retorted. 'We can't run from these things anymore.'

'I've seen them as well,' Taylor put in. 'I've seen them do what they do. One of them killed two of my friends. I know what they're capable of. This isn't something we can run away from anymore. We need to fight back against them.'

'I understand this,' Fraser observed. 'I've lost two valuable workers because of these phantoms.' He spoke of sour remorse and sadness. He deeply regretted and felt incredibly guilty still for sending Mike and Cameron to their deaths over some flour sacks.

'They were good people,' Fraser continued, 'that didn't deserve where they ended up. Given what we have had to go through already, I suggest that we need to stand with this guy. It does not matter what he has done, said or caused. He is a good man and follows his beliefs. We need to put aside those differences and fight back against these haunting terrors before we fall into subjugation. The horror has damaged our beloved Maysville and needs to come to an end.'

'It does matter what he has done,' boomed a well-known voice from the mist behind them. The entourage turned to see the damaged Commissioner Thorpe wheel up in his wheelchair to the guys around the burning bin. His officers, Love and Cruise, advanced slowly, with one officer standing on each side. They were armed with revolvers and pointed them towards the disgraced policeman and those he stood with. They held their breath, waiting for the order to kill. 'Did you really think that you were ahead of us?' Love sneered. 'Firing you was just a tiny first step in destroying you and keeping this place as it is.'

'This lunatic has caused pain and suffering. He needs to be stopped before he wrecks this entire village,' Thorpe declared.

'You caused this yourself when you tried to kill Father Carrey,'

Maguire snarled. 'This was your own fault, boss. You only know half of the story of what these ghosts want. Destroying the church would never have stopped the haunting of Sean Diaz. It would have made it even worse. With the church destroyed, he could go anywhere he wants. He will find other places to reign in fear.'

'You are a fool!' Thorpe barked furiously, his face blistering bright purple. 'You are as mad as those spirits you talk of that don't exist. You should have been locked up with that Churchwarden. All of you who are still alive when the sun is next in the sky will be facing jail time and will never see the light of day again. You will pay for what you have done to me: what you have done to this peaceful village.'

'Well, if that is how you want to play it, then you'll have to catch us first,' Maguire snapped. With that, he gave a violent shove and brutal punch in the direction of Cruise, knocking him to the muddy floor. He then led everyone as fast as he could. 'This way!' He screamed his loudest scream ever. They ran with him away from the corner until they reached the large water fountain in the centre of the village. However, the humiliated Commissioner had them in his grasp and had surrounded every possible exit around the fountain and was ready to see them all die. The group panicked with no sight of escape. They held hands together as they saw the three policemen advance towards them.

'Are you sure about this?' Taylor whispered as the arresting officers stood two feet from them. They looked like they could bite their heads off at the snap of their fingers. 'If they get us, we will be going down on every charge they can come up with. You know that, don't you?'

'I'm not really sure about anything at this point,' Maguire whispered back. 'We are in a world of spectral shit. We always have been.'

'Nothing about this has made any sense. And now our own humanity has turned against us and is ready to offer us up to the undead like they do not have enough legions already. There is nothing we can do. But it does not have to end that way. It does not mean we cannot go down with dignity and a fighting spirit. I wouldn't have missed this experience for the world, and I'm glad I could've helped,' Taylor said as bravely as she could.

'They can do what they want with us, just as long as they let the undead live their afterlives in peace,' Maguire replied. He closed his eyes as tight as a drum and expected a set of metal handcuffs to be placed around his wrists, crushing his last ounce of respect in the village. But, instead of the sound of those authoritative handcuffs clicking into place, he heard a burst of demonic laughter in their place. He realised who it belonged to. He opened his eyes to see a ghostly hoard. In the centre of them, Sean Diaz's spirit emerged.

'Glad you could join me for the end of the world,' Diaz snarled. 'At my side, these ghosts will take their rightful place as rulers of this planet. If anyone dares try to stand in our way, they will be struck down like a tree hit by lightning. Then they will be forced to suffer alongside us.'

'Disembodied rulers over a planet of humans?' Love scoffed aloud. 'I would like to see you try.'

'Oh really, doubtful fool,' Diaz scowled. 'Meet my undead followers.' He snapped his bony fingers. Several phantoms surrounded the policeman, conjuring a fire spell around him. Love suddenly burst into flames before the eyes of those humans in attendance.

'JESUS CHRIST!' Cruise gasped. He knelt down, gazing at the dusty remains of his incinerated partner. 'What the everlasting hell are we seeing? We've bitten off more than we can chew, and now we are paying the price for what we have ignored.'

'Let us hope Carrey didn't hear that,' Bruce sniggered. He often made strange remarks during tense emotions despite how tough he appeared.

'That is the price of ignorance,' Sean warned. 'It is pointless to fight us. Do not attempt it.' The ghost then fired a bolt of lightning from his hands, which struck Maguire in the centre of his stomach. The blast made everyone let go, and the circle was broken. Maguire fell to his knees in excruciating pain. But before he could succumb to the electrical execution, another spirit emerged from behind the team.

'Hold it, you devil,' the newcomer boomed. Diaz ceased his torturous methods and turned to face the spirit of Wet Jim. He saw the ghost walk out of the water in the fountain and step down on the floor opposite the bemused ghost before him. Maguire breathed a heavy sigh of relief. It was hard to do, given how long he was being tortured with the shame of being fired and the angst of being cursed like the ghosts. Taylor tried to soothe him as he stood tall.

Even stranger events were to follow in this horrific stand-off against the undead of Main Street.

'Diaz, this is where it ends for you and me now,' Jim hissed like a snake ready to clamp down on the mouse that was his ghostly enemy. 'It is time that you paid for what you did to me, what you have done to everyone I loved. Did you really think you were always going to be protected in the afterlife? Well, you cannot think about that anymore. Your time has come. You cannot escape justice now.'

Maguire came to a realisation. 'So, you were the one who murdered Jim. You murdered your sister's lover and then her?' he guessed.

'Silence, mortal!' Sean thundered furiously at the disgraced former captain. 'His demise was his own illegitimate fault,' he continued to gloat. 'He had an affair with my sister and ruined the lives of our family, tarnishing our name, spoiling our future, and sending my parents to an early grave. He did this to himself, and all you can do is try to defend this disgrace of a human being.'

'Did that give you any reason to kill the only sister you had?' Taylor asked in a serious tone.

Sean Diaz ignored this question from the young lady as he advanced towards the other spectre with a murderous glare in his eye. 'Even the afterlife would be far better off without a clueless snake like you,' he growled at Wet Jim. Both of the ghosts went for each other and fought swiftly and violently on the water of the fountain. They were at each other's throats as they tried to drain the energy from both. The human onlookers were in a state of panic as the fight was unfolding. The street had never seen so much of a brutal Halloween like this.

'If they fight this way any longer, they could tear this place apart into a living hell,' Maguire shuddered. He continued to stand well back as he wiped a trickle of blood away from his mouth using a dirty hanky in one hand whilst reaching for a branch with the other.

'Then we are doomed,' Thorpe gulped. He slunk back in his wheelchair with a stomach full of sin.

'So now you believe us?' Fraser asked. He stared down at the villainous superior officer cowering in his own selfish guilt. The businessman felt sorely tempted to shove him out of his wheelchair yet decided not to stoop to his appalling behaviour.

Just then, as the fighting intensified to levels of sure and certain death, there was a great flash of light billowing across the area, as if someone had turned on a bright lightbulb in their faces, blinding them thickly as the fighting ceased temporarily. Everyone looked towards the light to see the figure of a heavenly-shaped woman appear and take confident strides out of the strange light. She appeared to be wearing a white dress, similar to a wedding dress, herself having beautiful long brown hair and glowing eyes of the same colour. Her lips were as red as a ripe tomato, and her skin looked soft to the touch. She instantly beamed down from the heavens above them and powerfully advanced forward and divided both of the spirits as to stop their fighting. She stood in the middle of the yard so she could address everyone as if to give a speech.

Maguire squinted his eyes so as not to be blinded by the light. Then, he looked a little closer at the shape of the person arriving in this scene. He looked carefully at a photo linked to the case. He felt he had recognised the identity of the third spirit.

'Jennifer? Jennifer Diaz? The girl killed by the brother. Is that really you?' He asked.

'It is!' She addressed. 'I am finally glad that someone can recognise me when no one in my lifetime would bother to. I was summoned here from the nether world to end this haunting terror of Main Street once and for all and to bring home the men I loved, Jim and my brother. So that they may be at peace everlasting and forgive the evils of each other, leaving this Earth in a safe, incorrupt place once again.'

The legion of ghosts surrounding the mortal humans recognised this plea for the sanctuary of their better natures and knelt down at the bare feet of this peace-giving spirit, willing to repent and accept guidance where it was needed. They dropped their supernatural weapons and chose to surrender and bowed their heads to this figure with her amazing power of love and compassion.

Without a second thought of what she had suggested, they decided to let go of their hatreds and walk away from the world of the living and enter peaceful heaven. However, the inspiring words would not be enough given that Jim and Diaz had different opinions over her actions.

'She is right, Diaz,' Wet Jim pleaded. 'I am sorry for what I did to you and your family. And for what it had caused you to do. But now is not the time to fight over our evils and sins. We have been through so much over the last few years, fighting invisibility besides these blind mortals. We need to put our differences aside and return home to a place that is not forbidden.'

Diaz was having none of this begging for a better life. He held his villainous ground against the resolutions.

'You can try to appeal to a better nature, but you waste your time knowing that there is no better nature of mine to reach out for,' he declared. 'I am a forbidden soul and am twisted with evil as such. I am not prepared to leave this world like the coward that you are, Jim. I will have my promised rule over this dominion one way or another, even if you, or these mortal fools, choose not to stay.'

With no way to reason with the villainous being in any way, and with no hope of getting any repentance from him through another attempt of begging and appealing, Jim decided not to respond and let the phantom of Sean Diaz vanish into the darkness, uphold his terror of and across the Main Street and carry on with his torment for the rest of eternity. There was no other option left but to accept his powerful hatred of the world. Jim held out his hand for his dead lover to grasp, which she did. Her ghostly light spilled out into him, going straight through his ghostly body. He, too, became heavenly. He was happy to have gained redemption in a small way. He turned towards the humans grouped together.

'I am sorry for what I did to your friends, Taylor,' he said. 'I had no idea what I was doing given the amount of time I have spent in this realm. I also think Brendan needs to be sorry for how he has acted, especially as far as killing the Judge in the public house.'

Maguire's ears pricked up. 'You did what?' He glared towards his former boss with an angry glare.

'I think you just lost your job and your liberty,' Cruise gulped. Firmly realising that the game was up with the whole corruption charade, he came to his senses and turned his weapon on his disabled superior. 'It's time you go up on the charges. The same goes for me. For what I have done in this mess under your orders. Justice must always fit everyone, and no one is above the law. Not even the police themselves.'

'As long as you are willing to admit what you have done to me, the village and the Judge, you have earned my respect, even though there will be consequences,' Maguire stated. 'Justice exists to serve everyone. It will come in many forms, roles, and positions. What matters is how you make it work for others and work for yourself. Something the Commissioner clearly forgot about.'

'Shut it!' Thorpe growled. But whatever he ordered his minion to do was pointless, as Cruise placed a set of handcuffs around the Commissioner's wrists. Cruise declared his part in the whole affair and confessed to his sins. He knew he would suffer the same punishment as the commanding officer. But he didn't really care about that, just as long as he could feel absolved of his wrongdoings.

'All of this aside,' Jim continued. 'I would like to thank you for saving my soul and allowing me to rest in peace. You have done a great service to those in the world of the undead. Heaven will be glad to have you when it is your turn to pass.'

'Our pleasure,' Bruce commented as he got onto his motorbike. 'Go with God,' he said as he waved.

'Make sure you say hello to Kath for me,' Maguire said. He still felt sad about losing a valuable colleague. 'She was a great person in life and deserved a whole lot better than what Maysville had to offer her. Make sure she is well looked after.'

'You could always do that yourself,' Jennifer suggested. With these words, she waved her hand as if it was a magic wand. A whirlpool opened up beside the water fountain. The figure of a woman was revealed, along with the two other people killed in the floury van. The deceased policewoman advanced out of a whirlwind of smoke. There she was: flesh and blood. Resurrected.

Kath staggered towards Maguire and wrapped her arms around him. She felt very traumatised by what had been done. Maguire pulled her close to her, thinking briefly how wonderful it would be to tell these three people's families that they had all been returned safe and sound. Mike and Cameron rushed with open arms toward Fraser and Taylor, who both stood in silent shock. Their joyful team embrace seemed to last for years, although in reality, only minutes had passed before they pulled apart from each other, checking Mike and Cameron up and down to make sure it really was them and they really were alive.

'This is your kind reward for the great service you have done for us. Please take a moment to kindly accept it in good faith and take care of yourselves,' Jim said. 'It is time for us to move on from the troubled world. Goodbye, and thank you for your kind hearts. Always be sure to hold onto what you love and hold it tightly in your arms and heart. You may never know when it could be taken away from you.'

And with that, the spirit of Jim and his lover Jennifer ascended up to the top of the heavenly sky.

The onlookers gazed around the haunted remains of the village. The fighting was definitely over. But it did not feel like a victory to anyone present. The team looked around at the devastation that had been caused. It looked horrible.

'So, what do we do now?' Fraser asked. 'We have had so much

going on with these hauntings. We'll never be the same again.'

Maguire stared at Fraser and the rest of the team. 'Normally, you'd think I would accept Brendan's position as a secondary award for this crusade. But, in my present mind, not a chance. I am staying as a civilian for the rest of my life.'

'Sean's ghost could still be out there,' Bruce acknowledged. 'He has the power to destroy and enslave us in his reign of terror.'

The former police Captain looked around at everyone near him. He thought long and hard about their futures and fates if they remained in the haunted village. He knew that this had always been an evil place, ever since hearing about the first haunting with the beheaded Lord. Eventually, he came to realise that there was only one feasible way to put an end to the terror and nightmares for everyone.

'I do not see any other choices to make with this, guys,' he finally commented, a trickle of sweat falling across his forehead. He took a long deep breath of purely fresh air as he turned to his firm friends before he could say the following deadly order:

'We are going to have to permanently close and pull the village down to the ground, including the Main Street.' He took an even longer breath after he had said those controversial words knowing how horrific they sounded to the audience. Everyone in the torched area was not prepared for this statement to come out of his trembling mouth. They held their breaths for his explanation into this final idea.

'I see this to be the only way left in which we can stop the terror from carrying on. I think that if we take down the village, we could at least stop the ghost of Sean Diaz from spreading further afield and rebuilding a ghost army, cutting him off from the outside world.'

'It's an understandable claim,' Cruise agreed. He could feel that this was the only method.

Fortunately, he had been filming the whole ordeal through a video camera on his mobile phone. The footage was surprisingly good. Maguire himself presented the footage of the night's events as straightforward evidence to Councilor Farrell. She was still recovering from being shot by the Churchwarden, soon having the stitches taken out. After finally believing what had occurred concerning the ghosts, she reluctantly agreed to the demolition.

It was the hope that this demolition would put an end to the nightmare once and for all.

Epilogue

We now come to the final part of the story. It took a few days, but the demolition team soon arrived.

They set to work immediately, and Maysville and the Main Street were eventually pulled to pieces. It was not too long before the once prosperous village was reduced to a pile of rubble and dust sitting on the edge of the United Kingdom. Every building was toppled to the ground. There was literally nothing left.

Maguire had driven up to the gigantic hilltops to see the last of the village's destruction. It hurt him deep inside, with every toppling building, to look at what was happening to this place he used to call home, even for the shortest time. His place of hope and solace now corrupted by unjust rule and destroyed out of hatred, fear, and unrest.

Taylor sat beside him and watched him with a heavy heart. She handed him a handkerchief for him to wipe the sweat and tears of regret from his face. There was certainly a lot of each covering his worn-out face. He had not taken a wash in a long while, and it was beginning to look a lot more noticeable now that his life was tearing open again. There was a large drinks carton in the cup holder containing coffee. The girl passed it over to him, which he quickly drank. When he was done, he threw the carton out of the car window into a bin on the edge of the road.

'So now what do we do?' she asked. 'All of us have lost our home. Most of these people have nowhere to go. Where do we go from here?'

'I really don't know,' Maguire sighed. 'I suppose we could go anywhere we want. We have our freedom returned. Try again in new places across this country and the world. Perhaps we could learn some new things about each other as we begin our new lives.'

And this would prove to be true for lots of the now-former residents of Maysville.

Many people, such as Bruce and Kirsten, made it to London and lived their best lives in the capital. Many others involved in the fightback against the terror had the same idea, all living great lives, choosing to forget the horrors of the past. Bruce himself calmed down greatly in his thrill-seeking and found a good amount of peace with his emotions. He later went on to become a carpenter, working skillfully with his hands.

Mr Fraser rebuilt his business from the ground up and became a strong success again, perhaps even more than he had done before. He would later retire a wealthy and powerful man with a large legacy to his name.

Matt Cruise re-earned the respect of the police force. After a while in suspension and jail, he regained the trust of the police and got a good promotion in the force and succeeded as a strong and loyal policeman. Within two months, he amassed a brilliant arrest total and great respect. He told many other recruits his story and warned them of the perils of what abuses of power can cause.

The same, however, could not be said for his superior, Brendan Thorpe, who was jailed for life for his role in the ordeal.

'Where do you think that Sean Diaz will go now that this entire feud has come to an end?' Taylor asked with a worried expression. It was painfully obvious that Sean would never leave the site of Main Street without a lethal fight. Who knows, he might even be likely to return in the near future. 'He has no one to fight with anymore now that the people he killed have passed over to heaven.'

Maguire faced her with a mysterious glare in his eye. He had no idea what to think of this ghost's whereabouts, given how hard they were to predict. Who was he to speak for the actions of a spiteful homicidal spectre? What else could he be up to?

'Who can say?' He considered. 'Maybe he will go away with the destroyed village. One could only hope.

I suppose he will finally find a time to move on from the place that caused and fueled his pain and suffering for ages. Even I would find burning to death and then having to walk around seeking revenge exhausting. At least it's over now, and he can go away.

Perhaps he will soon find peace like all of us should. Given time, he will find that it is better to forgive and forget,' Maguire thought.

And on this note, Maguire started the engine of his green mustang. Without a moment to lose, they drove slowly away from the toxic remains of a ghostly life, abandoning how they had suffered, promising never to return to this hell, leaving in the hope that the terror on the Main Street of Maysville had finally come to its natural conclusion.

However, it is said that every Sunday night, every Halloween night and every misty, rainy night, the fearsome ghostly image of the evil Sean Diaz walks through the damaged countryside looking for fear to feast on, stalking those who failed him and the other ghosts.

When the moon is full and pure in the sky, he stands at the entrance of where the street once used to stand and where his reign of terror had begun, fearsome, gruesome, and silent. He looks out and acts as a grim warning to others wanting to investigate the horrific downfall he had caused. He is now suspended in time as a permanent protector for those who cannot find peace, just like him.

Plunging into the dark, screaming like a lost soul. Forever refusing to leave.

A short time later, the firmly retired Maguire was walking into a small corner shop. He picked up a number of groceries, fruit and vegetables, and a newspaper. He noticed a stain from a broken bottle of milk on the floor. Having gathered everything he needed, he then walked towards the counter. There was a young man in front of him waiting with a different-looking set of foods. They were standing beside a Halloween stand that was soon to be cleared to get ready for Guy Fawkes Night. He turned around to the former policeman.

'Do you know much about ghosts?' He asked. This question sounded very random in how it was delivered.

'Yes,' Maguire replied. 'You could say that I have had some experience. There can be many around these parts of the world,' he continued.

The young man said wistfully, 'I hope I can bring up my family into a world where they will not have to be scared of them at night. I would like to keep faith in this society in the hope that the world will keep them safe as we will. That they will live in perfect peace.'

'Quite so,' Maguire agreed. 'What is your family like?'

The young man smirked. 'It's a growing family. My wife is expecting a baby boy soon.'

'Good to hear,' Maguire smiled. 'Have you got a name for the little one?'

'We do indeed,' the young man declared. 'Wesley.'

THE END